D0405224

## ❧ SOCIETY WEDDINGS ❧

*His Majesty, the Sheikh of Gazbiyaa
Requests the honor of your attendance
at the royal wedding of*

*Zayed & Nadia*

*July 2015*

*At three o'clock in the afternoon*

*The Royal Palace Of Gazbiyaa*

*Reception immediately following
ceremony*

# ❧ SOCIETY WEDDINGS ❧

Dedicated bachelors Rocco Mondelli, Christian Markos, Stefan Bianco and Zayed Al Afzal met and bonded at university, wreaking havoc amongst the female population. In the decade since graduating, they've made their marks on the worlds of business and pleasure, becoming wealthy and powerful.

Marriage was never something Rocco, Christian, Stefan or Zayed were after...but things change, and now they'll have to do whatever it takes to get themselves to the church on time!

Yet nothing is as easy as it seems... and the women these four have set their sights on have plans of their own!

**Your embossed invitation is in the mail
and you are cordially invited to:**

The marriage of *Rocco Mondelli & Olivia Fitzgerald*
April 2015

The marriage of *Christian Markos & Alessandra Mondelli*
May 2015

The marriage of *Stefan Bianco & Clio Norwood*
June 2015

The marriage of *Sheikh Zayed Al Afzal & Princess Nadia Amani*
July 2015

*So RSVP and get ready to enjoy
the pinnacle of luxury and opulence
as the world's sexiest billionaires
finally say "I do."*

# Andie Brock

The Sheikh's Wedding Contract

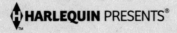

If you purchased this book without a cover you should be aware that this book is stolen property. It was reported as "unsold and destroyed" to the publisher, and neither the author nor the publisher has received any payment for this "stripped book."

ISBN-13: 978-0-373-13353-6

The Sheikh's Wedding Contract

First North American publication 2015

Copyright © 2015 by Harlequin Books S.A.

Special thanks and acknowledgment are given to Andie Brock for her contribution to the Society Weddings series.

Recycling programs for this product may not exist in your area.

All rights reserved. Except for use in any review, the reproduction or utilization of this work in whole or in part in any form by any electronic, mechanical or other means, now known or hereinafter invented, including xerography, photocopying and recording, or in any information storage or retrieval system, is forbidden without the written permission of the publisher, Harlequin Enterprises Limited, 225 Duncan Mill Road, Don Mills, Ontario M3B 3K9, Canada.

This is a work of fiction. Names, characters, places and incidents are either the product of the author's imagination or are used fictitiously, and any resemblance to actual persons, living or dead, business establishments, events or locales is entirely coincidental.

This edition published by arrangement with Harlequin Books S.A.

For questions and comments about the quality of this book, please contact us at CustomerService@Harlequin.com.

® and TM are trademarks of Harlequin Enterprises Limited or its corporate affiliates. Trademarks indicated with ® are registered in the United States Patent and Trademark Office, the Canadian Intellectual Property Office and in other countries.

Printed in U.S.A.

**Andie Brock** started inventing imaginary friends around the age of four and is still doing that today; only now the sparkly fairies have made way for spirited heroines and sexy heroes. Thankfully she now has some real friends, as well as a husband and three children, plus a grumpy but lovable cat. Andie lives in Bristol and when not actually writing, could well be plotting her next passionate romance story.

### Books by Andie Brock

### Harlequin Presents

*The Last Heir of Monterrato*

Visit the Author Profile page
at Harlequin.com for more titles.

To my daughter, Katherine. For her help and encouragement and most of all her patience! Thank you, Kit. x

# CHAPTER ONE

NADIA JUST HOPED she wasn't too late. As she neared the palace gates she could see groups of young women were already leaving, their diaphanous costumes fluttering as they hurried away, like colourful butterflies.

Inside the domed entrance to the palace she found herself being jostled by the departing throng of the harem, for that was what they were. The most beautiful women in the kingdom, bedecked and bejewelled, to be presented before the newly crowned Sheikh Zayed Al Afzal for his amusement and pleasure. Except that it seemed none of them had been deemed suitable. Had the sheikh dismissed them all, finding none of them good enough for his high and mighty standards? Certainly by the forbidding look on the guards' faces, the way they were herding the woman from the palace, it would appear that something had gone very wrong.

Well, she would just have to try harder. Ducking down, Nadia snatched up a fistful of the gauzy material of her skirt and, making herself as small as possible, started to dodge between the legs of the departing guests. She made it to the doorway and luck was with her as the eyes of the towering bodyguard were momentarily distracted by the exposed curves of a departing guest.

This was her chance. She started to run madly, breathlessly, along the wide hallway, her sandals squeaking on the marble floor, the bracelets on her arms and ankles and the heavily jewelled belt around her hips all jangling in a cacophony of giveaway noise.

There was an open door in front of her and blindly she ran towards it, with no plan in her head other than that she must not be stopped. She had to get in to see Sheikh Zayed Al Afzal.

Skidding to a halt, she found herself in the middle of an enormous glittering stateroom. And there, seated on a gilded throne on a raised dais at the far end of the room, was Sheikh Zayed.

They stared at one another. With her breath heaving, Nadia felt the hated bra top cutting into her and accentuating the swell of her breasts, her stomach muscles contracting beneath the jewelled belly button, her whole body exposed in a hideous betrayal of everything she believed in.

And she had certainly got his attention. She could feel the sheikh's eyes raking over her semi-naked body, her skin prickling with heat and self-consciousness in the wake of his sweeping gaze.

She knew this was her moment, her one chance, and she had to make it pay. But still she faltered. For this Sheikh Zayed was not what she had been expecting at all. He was tall and strikingly handsome, his long legs stretched out in front of him, crossed at the ankles. He wore a dark Western suit with elegant ease, and as Nadia raised her eyes she took in the broad expanse of his chest, the white shirt, the tie roughly pulled to one side. His hands, she noticed, were gripping the lions' heads on the arms of the throne, at odds with his relaxed posture.

Make eye contact, that was what she had to do now. Taking in a short, brave breath, she tipped back her head and braced herself to meet his gaze full on. She could do this. But what she saw was so much worse than she'd thought. For what halted the breath in her throat, sent her determination skittering sideways, was not the cruel eyes of the heartless killer she was expecting but something far more dangerous. They were beautiful eyes, a deep, dark chocolate brown, steady, assured and all seeing. The sort of eyes that could melt you. The sort of eyes that could snare you.

Suddenly she registered the laboured breath of a bodyguard behind her, but it was too late, his vice-like grip digging into the flesh of her forearm before she had any chance to dodge out of his way.

'My apologies, sire, this one slipped past us.'

This one? How dare he speak about her like that? Furiously trying to shake off his grasp, Nadia felt it tighten still farther. 'I'll thank you to take your brutish hands off me!'

The guard hesitated for a second, Nadia still squirming in his grasp.

'You heard what the lady said.' Rising to his feet, Zayed positioned himself on the edge of the dais. 'Let her go.' The words echoed around the vast chamber of the room.

'Sire.' The hand was released and the guard took a small step back and bowed his head.

'And for future reference, I expect my orders to be carried out in a civilised manner. Let it be known that I will not tolerate brutality in any form.'

'Your Royal Highness.'

Nadia turned to give the admonished guard a haughty stare, pointedly rubbing at the red marks he had made on her arm. The wretched bangles jangled.

'So, young lady.' As he swiftly turned his attention to her Nadia felt the spotlight of Zayed's glare. 'What is your name?'

'Nadia.' She delivered it clearly enough but said out loud it made her feel all the more exposed.

'Well, Nadia, I'm afraid I have to inform you that you have had a wasted journey.' He stood tall and proud, with his legs apart and his arms crossed over his chest, very much the master of control. 'You see, I am not in the habit of choosing my companions in the way that has been arranged tonight. I must apologise for inconveniencing you.'

Somehow it sounded more like a reprimand than an apology.

'But, Your Royal Highness…' With her heart thudding in her chest she raised her eyes to meet his, opening them as wide as she could before lowering them again and batting her dark lashes in what she hoped was a seductive gesture. 'Since I am here, may I not be allowed to perform for you?' Without waiting for an answer she slowly, hesitantly, began to make her hips sway, undulating them in the way she had seen the dancers perform in her own palace, for the entertainment of her father and brother.

She had studied them as closely as she could from her hiding place in the shadowed recesses of the palace ballroom, committing the movements to memory before hurrying back to her bedroom to practise what she had seen. Trying not to look her reflection in the eye, she had disrobed to her underclothes and gyrated earnestly before the mirror. Now she just needed to try to remember what she had learned.

She raised her arms above her head, twisting her hands around each other in the seductive, trance-like way she had seen performed, her hips moving more provocatively now as the moves came back to her, the jewelled beads jingle-jangling as she shimmied her behind first one way, then the other, her feet lightly moving beneath her.

'Young lady.' Zayed had descended the few steps from the dais and was striding across the brightly coloured mosaic floor towards her. Nadia's dancing became more and more daring as she took her humiliation and turned it into raw sensuality, undulating her stomach and gyrating her hips with an excruciating lack of abandon.

He was right in front of her now. So tall, so close, his

dark shape towering over her as he looked down at her overheated, increasingly desperate dancing.

Still Nadia didn't stop, her eyes now level with his broad chest, her arms spiralling wildly in front of his face.

'I obviously haven't made myself clear.' Suddenly his strong hands had caught hers in midair and he lowered them slowly down to her sides, his eyes not leaving her flushed face. All movement ceased, apart from the shudder of shame that ran through Nadia. Raising his hands to her shoulders, he turned her, gently but firmly, in the opposite direction. 'The door is that way.'

Zayed watched as the beguiling young temptress scurried down the corridor, flanked by the guard, who was now thankfully keeping his hands to himself. She seemed keen to get away, her hurried strides rippling the long black curls down her back and making that particularly pert derrière sway alluringly beneath the tantalisingly flimsy costume. But the rest of her posture was stiff and aloof. Which seemed odd, when you considered her wanton performance just a few minutes before. The display she had just treated him to.

And a very nice display it had been, too, he had to say. There was no doubt that this Nadia was a beauty, the way she exhibited her pale-skinned flesh turning him on far more than he would admit to himself. If circumstances were different, if he were to come across her in a bar, for example, it would give him the greatest of pleasure to get to know her, in every sense of the word. But not here, not like that. He might have the reputation for being a womaniser, but seducing a beautiful woman was one thing. Having the poor creatures herded before him like a cattle market, quite another. Not that Nadia looked as if she would be easily herded anywhere. How she had ended up here was a mystery.

Scowling, Zayed turned away, and, shrugging off his

jacket, he threw it over his shoulder. Standing in the middle of the opulent stateroom, he looked around him. What the hell had happened to his life? A couple of months ago he had been expanding his business empire, travelling the world, loving the thrill of facilitating multibillion-dollar company takeovers and the wealth and trappings that went with being hugely successful at his job.

But all that had changed, dramatically so, when his mother had made the shock announcement that he was to return home, to the kingdom of Gazbiyaa. That *he*, Zayed, was to be crowned the next sheikh of Gazbiyaa, and not his elder brother, Azeed. The decision had been equally momentous for both brothers: Zayed thrown into the totally unfamiliar role of sheikh, something that he had never been prepared for, never expected and certainly never wanted, and Azeed, who had been groomed for this role all his life, having the title brutally snatched away from him.

Now the newly crowned Sheikh Zayed Al Afzal, supreme ruler of the fabulously wealthy desert kingdom of Gazbiyaa, gazed bitterly around the empty room. He was going to have to make some serious changes round here, and fast, assert his authority before he was subjected to any more hideous debacles like the one tonight. A harem indeed. What on earth had that been about?

He only wished he could have stopped it before the poor women had arrived. The first he'd known of it was when one of his advisors had ushered him into the stateroom with a sweeping gesture of the arm and announced that the most beautiful women in the kingdom were waiting to be selected for his entertainment. Momentarily stunned, he had only been able to stare in disbelief as the room had filled with these bejewelled creatures, their eyes flashing, their bodies twirling as they paraded before him. By the time he had come to his senses and ordered that they be removed his voice had become raised and his anger all too obvious, making him come across as some sort of brutish tyrant. He was ashamed to remember the frightened look in their eyes as they were rounded up and told to leave. Because his anger wasn't meant for those poor girls, it was aimed at himself. For the position he had been forced to accept and the crazy life he now found himself in.

But that last young woman, Nadia—that certainly hadn't been fear in her eyes. Her parting glance, blazing over her shoulder as she'd left, had been full of mystery and challenge, with a dollop of haughty imperiousness for good measure. Suddenly he found himself trying to remember the colour of those remarkable eyes. Dark blue? Violet?

Pulling himself up short, Zayed took a sharp breath and turned to stride from the room. Why was he wasting his time trying to figure that out? Didn't he have bigger things to worry about?

Nadia felt the cold night air brush over her heated skin and shivered violently. What now? That gorilla of a guard had escorted her to the palace gates without a word, locking them firmly behind her, and now she watched his retreating figure through the bars as he ascended the long flight of steps back up to the entrance, where he would no doubt take up his position to make sure she didn't slip past him again.

Well, she would just have to come up with another plan. One thing was for sure, she wasn't going to give up now. Not now she had been inside the palace and met Sheikh Zayed Al Afzal face-to-face. Although *met* was hardly the right word. The look of disgust on his face as he had turned her from the room after her little performance still produced a cringe that would buckle her body if she let it. Which she wouldn't.

But along with the humiliation, there was no doubt that this formidable sheikh had made another, more un-expected, impression on Nadia. Tall, broad shouldered and commanding—all these things she had taken in in an instant. But there was more: a quiet intelligence, an urbane sophistication that, coupled with his extreme good looks, was a heart-stopping combination. Certainly he was like no man Nadia had ever come across before. And certainly he had made her feel something she had never felt before. Something she had no intention of thinking about now.

Crossing her arms over her chest, Nadia rubbed at the chilly exposed flesh of her shoulders while she studied the vast palace that was now tantalisingly out of her reach. The epitome of extravagant opulence, it glowed against the night sky, each of its numerous arched windows, porticos and colonnades floodlit a fiery amber, the enormous blue dome in the centre of the roof pierced by the illuminated crescent moons. It looked unreal in this light, like a shining UFO that had landed in the desert.

Nadia was no stranger to palace life; in fact it was the only life she had ever known. Born Princess Nadia Amani of Harith, she had spent her entire twenty-eight years a virtual prisoner in the palace of Harith, confined by the archaic rules of protocol and the equally archaic rules of her father and brother. But the palace that she had grown up in, that she knew so well, seemed very humble in comparison to the magnificent edifice before her now. The palace of Gazbiyaa left no one in any doubt of the mighty wealth and power of this kingdom.

But if growing up in a palace had taught Nadia one thing, it was that there was always a way in. She just had to find it. She was about to move away to start her search when movement at one of the windows on the fourth floor caught her eye. Retreating into the shadows, even though there was no way she could be seen down here, she watched as the French windows were pushed open wide and she could just make out the silhouette of Zayed himself, framed against the light. Were these the sheikh's private quarters? Silently, Nadia counted one, two, three, four windows from the central portico. Committing the image to memory, she felt her heart start to thud in her chest again. This was where she had to head to commit the bravest, most dangerous and possibly the stupidest act of her life. But first she had to find her way in.

Leaning on the balcony railings outside his bedroom window, Zayed breathed in the sweetly scented night air. Before him stretched the kingdom, his kingdom, spread out like a twinkling tapestry. The recently erected skyscrapers soared into the sky, the daring glass and steel monuments that pushed the boundaries of architects' dreams and construction workers' abilities to the limit and beyond, each one taller, more daring, more dazzling than the last. This had been his brother's dream, to make the kingdom of Gazbiyaa a major player, not just in the Middle East, but on the world stage. But at what cost? Azeed was ruthless and determined, and Zayed suspected that had Azeed been crowned sheikh he would have stopped at nothing in his quest to make Gazbiyaa the ultimate superpower.

And that was why Zayed's mother had broken her vow of silence on her deathbed, putting an end to Azeed's increasingly extreme plans and precipitating the chain of events that had led to Zayed standing here now.

Through the buzz of the city traffic Zayed could hear the call to prayer, floating from the dozens of minarets that were dotted about the city landscape, dwarfed in size by their towering neighbours but still more than making their presence felt.

Turning back from the window, Zayed headed for the bathroom to take a shower. It had been a long day.

It was the azan, the call to prayer, that gave Nadia her chance. She had followed the wall round to the back of the palace, where to her dismay she saw that the gates were just as high, just as impenetrable, when a small group of young men appeared, hurrying towards her, their robes glowing white in the dusky light. Shrinking into the shadows, Nadia watched as one of them touched a keypad and the gates opened, allowing them to pass through. She had just enough time to slip in behind them before they silently slid closed again.

With her heart in her throat she kept to the shadows as she hurried towards the brightly lit palace, past the manicured lawns and rows of swaying palm trees, the vast courtyard dotted with fountains, until she was within a few hundred yards of the kitchens. Here she stopped, squatting down behind a pomegranate tree to catch her breath and try to figure out what to do next.

A solitary male voice alerted her to a palace guard talking into his mobile phone in front of the kitchen doors. The open kitchen doors. She just needed to distract him. A plan started to form in her head; she hadn't idled away her years watching adventure movies on the television for nothing. Feeling around her feet, she found what she was looking for and, picking up the smooth pomegranate, she felt its weight in her hand. If she could just throw it somewhere away to the side of that guard, it might distract him long enough for her to slip in.

Slipping the bracelets off her wrist and discarding them, she stood up and took aim, flinging the pomegranate wildly and with all her might as hard as she could. The result was better than she could ever have imagined. By some luck the weighty fruit landed square on the bonnet of a sleek black limousine she hadn't even noticed, and as its alarm shrieked into life the guard immediately hurried over to investigate. This was her chance. Nadia sprinted towards the open door and she was in!

Casting around her in exhilarated panic, she saw that

luck was with her again and the kitchens appeared to be completely empty. Tiptoeing through one room after another, she eventually found the servants' staircase and started to climb it with the feverish speed and blind panic born of doing something very, very dangerous.

By the time she reached the fourth floor she was almost doubled over with the exertion, but she couldn't allow herself more than a couple of gasping breaths. She peeped out into the long corridor. All seemed quiet, though it wasn't easy to tell over the banging of her own heartbeat and the roaring in her ears. Raising shaky hands to her temples, she tried to get her bearings, turning this way and that in an attempt to figure out where she was. Four windows from the central portico at the front. If she followed this passageway to the end, turned left and then counted the doors…

Her hand was on the doorknob now. If her calculations were right she was about to enter the bedchamber of Sheikh Zayed Al Afzal. Slowly, slowly she turned the heavy brass knob. It moved silently, readily beneath her grasp. There was no going back now. Whatever fate awaited her on the other side of this door, she knew her life would never be the same again.

Zayed was towelling himself dry when he heard a noise coming from his bedchamber next door. He froze, the towel in his hand. Someone was in there, he was sure of it. He strained his ears to listen but there was no sound now.

But a sixth sense told him that he was no longer alone. Had he locked his bedroom door? No, of course he hadn't. Despite warnings that security was of paramount importance here, he couldn't break the habit of a lifetime. Who, in the civilised world, locked their door before going to bed? Unless they didn't want to be disturbed for a very different reason, of course.

Now he certainly wished he had heeded the advice.

His eyes scanned the bathroom for some sort of weapon, anything he could use to defend himself, but it was hopeless. A bottle of shower gel and a loofah was about as lethal as it got. He would just have to use his wits and his own muscle. He was strong and he was fit and he knew how to disarm an attacker, especially with the element of surprise. If there was only one intruder, even if they were armed, he could do this. More than that? He would give it his best shot. Tucking the towel around his waist, he inched forward.

Creeping into the bedchamber, Nadia sucked in a breath and held it there, too terrified to let it out. In front of her was an enormous raised bed, the interior obscured by a canopy of sumptuous drapes that fell from a gilded corona above.

Was he in there? Tiptoeing closer, wincing with every silent footstep, Nadia reached forward and with a clammy hand shakily drew back the fabric a couple of inches. The bed was empty. He must be in the bathroom. The breath finally escaped from her lungs. This was it. All of her carefully laid plans had led to this point. Slipping off her sandals, she climbed into the bed as quietly as she could. Then, squirming on top of the satin sheets, she tried to arrange herself in a vaguely alluring position before lying back against the pillows with her eyes screwed shut. She was ready for her fate.

There was a noise, a sort of low animal growl, followed by a flash of muscled chest and the purposeful swing of arms through the air. And the next thing Nadia knew, she was being pinned to the bed by the considerable weight of over six feet of powerful, adrenaline-fuelled, near-naked flesh.

# CHAPTER TWO

'WHO ARE YOU and what do you want?' Zayed snapped the words into Nadia's ear, her head twisted into the pillow, a tangle of black curls obscuring the side of her face.

She couldn't speak, couldn't breathe come to that. With her arms wrenched above her head, both wrists shackled by Zayed's forceful grasp, the shock and fear that were pumping through her body were threatening to make her lose consciousness completely. Slowly, deliberately, she tried to turn her head, hoping that once Zayed saw that it was just her, Nadia, he would release her, give her a chance to explain. Although she wasn't sure how she was going to do that.

But what she saw soon put paid to any such fanciful notions. Because the dark brown eyes that she found herself staring into, just inches away from her face, were still glittering with intent, ready to attack. Everything about his forbidding face, the clench of his jaw beneath the closely cropped beard, the dark, untidy brows drawn together in a menacing scowl, the tight line of his lips, told her she was in big trouble. He was going to kill her, wasn't he? She was going to die. Murdered in a stranger's bed, then chopped into small pieces and offered as tasty morsels to the palace falcons.

'It's only me.' She gulped noisily, her eyes wide with panic. 'Nadia.' She wriggled beneath him to try to free some small part of her trapped body, any part, but the movement simply increased the contact between them and she stopped abruptly. That clenching spasm, somewhere low down where their bodies met, that had to be fear, didn't it?

'I know quite well who you are.' Zayed's breath swept hot and dry across her face. 'But what I don't know is why the hell you are in my bed.' Anger seethed in his voice and his grip tightened still farther around her wrists. 'I want an answer, now.'

'Your Royal Highness.' Fighting to find her voice that was crushed somewhere down with the rest of her body, Nadia now lay very still, blinking her wide violet eyes at her fearsome captor. Her only chance of survival was to try to talk herself out of this mess. 'I can assure you, I mean you no harm. I merely felt the overwhelming need to see you again.'

'Yeah, of course you did.' Sarcasm cut through his voice and as he shifted his weight on top of her Nadia felt an alarming rush of blood sweep through her. 'Not good enough, I'm afraid. Who are you working for and what do you want?'

'No one, really. I am completely alone.'

'I don't believe you.' His voice was a hoarse whisper against her skin. 'Are you here to distract me? Is that it? Keep me occupied while an accomplice creeps in to slit my throat?' Locking his arms now, he raised his bare chest enough to twist round to look over his shoulder, as if the assailant might already be there, brandishing a knife, before lowering it back down over Nadia's breasts. Nadia's eyes widened. The movement had shifted his weight, the jut of his hips, the meeting of their groins.

'No, nothing like that, I just—'

'Or my father's throat? Is that was this is about? I know my father has many enemies.'

'No. You have to believe me. I'm not here to slit any-one's throat.'

Chance would be a fine thing. With her arms pinned above her on either side of her head, her breasts stretched taut and high beneath the rock-hard pressure of Zayed's chest, she couldn't have felt more vulnerable, more laid bare. And worse than that, with Zayed's full weight on top of her, the whole length of his virtually naked body bearing down on her, his masculine heat trapping her be-neath him, she was aware of a growing ache, low down in her belly, that had nothing to do with the pressure of his weight alone. She drew in a ragged breath, but it was full of the scent of him, the heady mixture of musky shower gel and pumping pheromones.

'So just what are you doing here, Nadia?' Zayed's face lowered down again, so close now that the space between them had almost vanished completely. His fearsome fea-tures blurred out of focus as his mouth hovered over hers and he whispered, 'You have exactly one minute to tell me the truth.'

'And I will.' Nadia bit down hard on her lip to try to get some control. 'When you have released me.'

'Uh-uh,' Zayed grated. 'That's not how it works.' He tipped back his head. 'You tell me the truth now, or I call the palace guards.'

'No! Don't do that.' Her attempt at defiance immedi-ately crumbled.

This was so not what she had planned, to be pinned down on the bed like a common intruder. She was meant to be alluring, for heaven's sake. Leading him into temp-tation and a betrothal that would prevent their kingdoms going to war. That had been the plan, at least. Now that plan had been well and truly squashed, along with her poor body, and the man she was supposed to be seducing looked as if he would much rather throttle her than make love to her. But she had to be strong, try again. 'Before I tell you anything I demand that you let go of my wrists.'

'You demand, eh?' Zayed snorted. 'That's a good one. It may have escaped your notice but you are hardly in a position to make demands. I suggest you drop the high-and-mighty routine right now and come up with one good reason for me not to call the guards and have you clapped in irons and thrown into the palace dungeons. You have ten seconds and counting.'

'Okay, okay.' Nadia ran her tongue over her dry lips. 'I came here…' She could feel her heart hammering between them, hammering more violently with each decreasing second, feel the rough scratch of Zayed's chest hair, the sheen of sweat that sealed them. 'I came here quite alone, simply because I hoped… I hoped to be able to make you happy.' The last words came out in a rush as the ridiculousness of her statement hit home. One thing was for sure: this sheikh looked anything but happy.

'Time's up.'

'No, wait, really.' Pure desperation clawed at her throat. This was all going horribly wrong.

Alone in her bed in the palace of Harith she had made herself picture this moment, prepare herself, using every bit of courage and fortitude she could muster to help her get through the ordeal that she knew she was going to have to face.

She had convinced herself it would all be worth it. If her virginity was the price that had to be paid to halt the threat of war between the kingdoms of Harith and Gazbiyaa, then she would do it, a hundred times over. Because she loved her country, even though it didn't always feel as if her country loved her. And this crazy, dangerous, down-right perilous scheme was the only way she could see that she could make a difference.

But the heartless sheikh that she had imagined sacri-

ficing her honour for had turned out to be nothing like the
real-life version. The darkly handsome man who stared
down at her now, his eyes sharply focused on her face, his
jaw set with fierce determination, was altogether a much
more worrying proposition.

From what she had managed to glean from her father
and brother, she had gathered that the newly crowned
sheikh was nothing but a brutal, debauched hedonist, a
man who spent his time in bars and nightclubs drink-
ing alcohol and pursuing his only real interest: the plea-
sures of the female flesh. A man who had no regard for
his people or his country. For all his multibillion-dollar
business empire, he had none of the skills and knowledge
needed to rule a kingdom such as Gazbiyaa. Which was
why, like a hyena circling a vulnerable lion, Harith was
poised, ready to pounce.

But Nadia already knew her father and brother were
wrong about Zayed Al Afzal. Far from being the extravagant philanderer they had described, he was obviously a
highly intelligent man, sharp and shrewd and perceptive.
To underestimate him would prove cataclysmic for Harith.
For everyone.

And he didn't even appear to be interested in the plea-
sures of the flesh. Not hers anyway. She was the one whose
body was experiencing an unfamiliar ache beneath the
hard, warm, damp skin of her captor.

But who could blame her? The towel that was wrapped
around his lower torso was rubbing against her bare mid-
riff, his weight forcing the jewelled belt around her hips
to dig into her skin. She could feel the shape of him, the
bulge of this very male part of his anatomy, hot and intimate and completely impossible to ignore as it pushed
against her groin. It was driving every bit of any rehearsed
speech she might have had right out of her mind.

Sucking in a shallow breath, Nadia determinedly

squirmed beneath him in a last attempt to free herself. And she did feel him lift himself off her, just an inch or so, and just for a second. Taking full advantage, she bucked her hips, her breasts rising with her, hopeful that she might be able to unbalance him somehow. But as Zayed's weight closed the gap between them even more tightly than before, she realised her action had had a very different result. She gasped. His full-blown erection was pressing into her groin, straining between them like a rod of steel beneath its towel cover. As her eyes flew to his she caught the gleam of undiluted lust and her own eyes, reflected in his, mirroring his desire.

So she could do this to him. He wasn't totally impervious to her.

She squirmed again, revelling in this minor power she had over him, in the clenching, craving waves of sexual awakening that the feel of his rock-hard member had triggered in her.

Maybe her plan could still work. Maybe she could still tempt him into making love to her and start the chain of events that would eventually, somehow, achieve what this dangerous charade was all about—a lasting peace between their two nations. Just maybe.

But one thing was for sure. She had to make this moment count.

'Your Royal Highness—' she fixed her sultry, dark lilac eyes on his '—if you wanted to take me now I would not object. Whatever you should ask of me I will willingly provide and I would do my very best not to disappoint you.'

Instantly, the desire in Zayed's eyes vanished.

'Enough!' Finally freeing her wrists, he pushed his torso up, locking his elbows, so that he now looked down on her, scornful contempt burning in his eyes. 'Stop this horrible seduction routine. I can assure you I have no intention of *taking you*. That is most definitely *not* my style.'

Nadia slowly brought her arms down from over her head, lowering them awkwardly so that they didn't touch any part of his skin. She was fighting to stop his wounding words from showing on her face.

'I'll have you know I am not in the habit of having sex with someone just because they offer it to me. Especially duplicitous young women who sneak uninvited into my bed and then somehow think they can seduce me for their own gain. Whatever gain that might be.'

She stared at him in dismay. She had been sure that the way to beguile a powerful and ruthless ruler was to offer up the only thing that was truly hers to give—her virginity. The never-to-be-recovered gift of her virtue. Now, despite the obvious interest she had stirred in his body, it seemed a laughable idea.

To a man like Sheikh Zayed such a prize meant nothing. Quite the reverse, in fact. Why would he be interested in her when he could pick and choose from the most sophisticated women in the world, sexually experienced women, who would know exactly how to make him happy?

And more than that, here was a man with far too much integrity and morality to ever be tempted into having sex with someone just because he could; she knew that now. She had got it all wrong and now she was doomed, but to what fate she had no idea.

'I apologise, Your Highness.' She pushed the words past her choked throat. 'I can see that my behaviour has displeased you.'

'Can we dispense with the *Your Highness* bit?' Zayed cut sharply through her apology. 'I think it's fair to say that the situation we are in has bypassed the need for formal protocol. How about you just explain what the hell you are up to and I decide what to do with you?'

Both of those things sounded equally terrifying to Nadia. Screwing her eyes tightly shut, she tried to think of a way out of this mess. But when she opened them again Zayed was still staring down at her, waiting for her reply, and when he leaned forward with his hand raised she instinctively flinched.

'Good God, woman.' He stopped, appalled, twisting the black strand of her hair in his fingers. He had simply meant to brush it away from her heated face. 'What sort of brute do you think I am?'

Nadia shook her head. 'No, I don't…'

'What desperation would bring you to the bed of someone you obviously think would strike you?'

If only he knew. If only she could tell him the truth. But if she revealed who she was now, admitted that she was from Harith, she was certain he would instantly carry out his threat and have her clapped in irons and left to rot in the palace dungeons. That was the strength of hatred between the two kingdoms.

'I'm not letting you go until you tell me, Nadia.' His voice was low and grating, and she knew he was fighting to keep his patience, her silence obviously antagonising him even more. Shifting his weight, he leaned forward again, one muscled arm on either side of her head, his chest hovering just an inch above her own. 'I'm waiting.'

'Okay, okay, I will tell you. The reason I am here…'

Suddenly Nadia stopped, saved from having to continue by the sound of a brisk tap on the door behind them. Zayed hesitated, poised and alert. There was another tap.

'Your Royal Highness?' A male voice came through the door.

Zayed abruptly pulled his body off hers, and, pushing aside the drapes from the bed, got out. Turning away, he adjusted the towel around his hips before heading for the door. 'Stay here.' He hissed the order. 'I'll get rid of them.'

Nadia didn't intend to do any such thing. If this was her only chance of escape she was going to grab it. Leaping up, she started to scrabble on all fours across the slippery satin sheets to the edge of this enormous bed in a desperate bid for freedom.

'Oh, no, you don't.' She hadn't so much as got a foot to the floor before he was on her again, pushing her back against the pillows. Desperate now, Nadia bucked wildly beneath him, kicking her legs out to the side, wildly grabbing at anything she could get hold of. Which turned out to be a handful of Zayed's towel. As she inadvertently ripped it from his hips she caught a glimpse of tight, naked buttocks before his body closed down on hers again.

'Ahem.' A polite cough alerted them both to the presence of someone else in the room. 'Forgive me, Your Royal Highness.'

'Go away!' Furious, Zayed barked the words over his shoulder as he glared down at the now frozen Nadia.

'I do apologise, sire, but I come with a message.' There was another nervous cough. 'From your father, sire. I believe it is a matter of some importance.'

Nadia started at the sound of the key turning in the lock and quickly turned to face the door, her hands behind her back.

It was about half an hour since Zayed had imprisoned her in his bedchamber. Having pulled on a pair of jeans and a T-shirt, the quick flash of his naked rear widening Nadia's eyes still farther, he had locked the door to the interconnecting suite of rooms, theatrically jangling the bunch of keys in front of her face to make sure she had got the message. Finally, hissing a few curt words through his teeth to the effect that he would deal with her later, he had marched from the room, locking the door behind him.

Nadia's first thought was that there had to be some way to escape. After futilely rattling the door handles she had felt along the panelled walls, convinced that there had to be a hidden doorway somewhere. But if there was, it was too well hidden for her to discover. And one look at the terrifying drop from the fourth-floor windows had convinced her that, unless she could somehow sprout wings before she hit the ground, that wasn't an option, either.

So instead she had ended up pacing round the room, impotent fury pumping through her veins that she, Princess Nadia of Harith, should be held captive against her will by this maddening sheikh. Furious, too, that all her plans had gone so horribly wrong and she couldn't see any way out of this mess.

Her pacing had taken her over to a large ormolu-mounted desk in the corner of the room. A collection of electronic devices littered the top: a laptop, a smartphone, a tablet. Nadia had never been allowed any of these things, her brother insisting that they would be a corrupting influence on her. But it was the modestly framed photo at the back of the desk that caught her eye. Picking it up, Nadia studied the four fine young men wearing grey gowns and mortar boards and grinning widely for the camera. Graduation day. Four young men with the world at their feet. There was Zayed, second from the left with his arms slung over the shoulders of his friends, several years younger but already heartbreakingly handsome and a twinkle in his eye that said he knew it. Nadia felt something pull inside.

'What are you doing?'

'Nothing.' Nadia glared back at him, fumbling to replace the photo behind her on the desk. 'I'm hardly in a position to *do* anything, locked in here like a prisoner.'

'And whose fault is that?' He growled the words as he ran his hand over his thick dark hair. Nadia recognised the weariness of the gesture, sensed the heavy weight of responsibility that he carried, quite apart from the trouble she was causing him. She almost felt sorry for adding to his burden. Almost. 'You are damned lucky I haven't called security—' he paused '—yet.'

Nadia felt his eyes scanning her body again, starting with the bra top and sweeping down the length of her torso to her bare stomach that contracted under his gaze, lower to her belted hips and long, shapely legs that the sheer, gauzy fabric twisting around them made no attempt to conceal.

She squirmed visibly. Zayed cleared his throat.

'The question is, what do I do with you now?'

From the fierce look on his face Nadia suspected he wasn't waiting for an answer from her. And even if he had been she wasn't sure how to reply.

Despite her earlier determination to escape, she had no idea what she would do if she was set free, where she would go, especially still dressed in this hateful outfit.

Returning to Harith was out of the question. She knew that by now her disappearance would have sparked a full-scale search of the kingdom, that her father and brother would be seething with rage when she had not returned from the 'shopping trip' she had set out on earlier that morning, a morning that now seemed an eon ago. She knew that her mother would already be worried sick, and for that she was genuinely sorry. She would have loved to have been able to confide in her, tell her of her daring plan, but she knew that she couldn't. Years of persecution from her husband and then her son had weakened her mother from the highly intelligent, spirited young woman of her youth to the nervous, fearful woman she was today. Nadia had watched her decline, powerless to do anything about it. But one thing was for sure. She was never going to let that happen to her.

And so she had made her escape. Accompanied by her chaperone, a young woman called Jana whom Nadia had secretly befriended, she had set out with instructions to buy 'the fine clothes for her trousseau.' The money her family had given her for this task had been extremely generous and, added to the stash that Nadia had been accumulating over the past months, amounted to a small fortune.

In fact, she and Jana had only made one purchase of clothing, the harem outfit that the two nervously giggling young women had chosen hardly being what her family had had in mind. Then, taking just enough for her flight ticket to Gazbiyaa, Nadia had insisted that Jana had the rest of the money, and the two women had embraced long and hard before Jana had set off on her own adventure, fleeing back to her family with the money for her mother's operation tucked safely away beneath her hijab. Nadia just hoped she was having more luck than she was.

Zayed had walked across the room, positioning himself in front of one of the balcony windows with his arms folded across his chest, the middle finger of one hand tapping an impatient beat. Nadia could do nothing but silently watch as he decided what he was going to do with her.

'You know what—' he sighed heavily '—I could stand here all night, trying to figure out what you are doing here, why you have broken into my bedroom, sneaked into my bed. But frankly—' he stopped to give Nadia a particularly derisory stare that shrivelled her insides '—I don't even care.'

'Your Royal Highness, if I could just be allowed to explain—'

'No, Nadia.' Raising a firm hand, Zayed stopped her. 'I refuse to listen to any more of your *explanations*. I've heard more than enough of your half-baked nonsense for one evening. But, as much as I would like to be rid of you, I am not going to be held responsible for whatever fate might befall you walking the city streets at this time of night looking like that.'

The sneering gesture, along with the look of distaste

on his face that went with it, clearly spelled out just what he thought of her attire.

'You will stay tonight in the palace.'

As Nadia opened her mouth to protest he barked, 'And that's an order.'

Moving over to the marble-topped credenza, Zayed took out a bottle of Scotch and a crystal tumbler and poured himself a generous measure. Then, pulling out a chair, he sat down heavily, stretching his long legs out in front of him and flexing his muscled arms behind his head. This evening had to rank as one of the most bizarre of his life—and that was saying something.

When he had found out that he, rather than his brother Azeed, was to be crowned sheikh of Gazbiyaa, he had immediately known that his life would change dramatically and forever. He could never have foreseen the circumstances that had led to his being in this position, but the fact was that the future of the kingdom was now in his hands and duty to his country and his subjects had to come before everything else.

From a practical point of view he could do it, he knew that. He had absolute faith in his abilities. His hugely successful global company was a testament to his business acumen and he was certain he could further the prosperity of the fledgling but rapidly moving expansion of the kingdom's economy. More than that, his keen intelligence and insightful mind meant he instinctively made astute judgements, knowing just when to take the hard line or to follow a more diplomatic approach. Something that could only stand him in good stead with the role he now found himself in.

But emotionally he was still struggling to come to terms with the idea of being the sheikh of Gazbiyaa. This was not the life he had planned for, not the life he had ever wanted. And the more he saw of it, the less he liked it.

Because beneath the flashy, showy front that Gazbiyaa presented to the world, the front that he had let himself believe when he had been thousands of miles away in New York pursuing his own career, there was a bedrock of injustice and ignorance. Like a cloak of the finest gold brocade thrown over a rotting pit of wolves and snakes. What his father called honour and tradition he would term bigotry and prejudice, and the more closely he examined this place, the more deep-rooted he saw that it was. Something he knew he was going to have to address.

The conversation he had just had with his father had done nothing to lighten the load. It seemed that news had come through that Azeed, who had fled Gazbiyaa in a furious rage on learning he would never be crowned sheikh, was heading for the kingdom of Harith. And far from being a cause for relief that his exiled brother was safe and well, this had simply heightened the threat of war between the two kingdoms.

The conflict between Gazbiyaa and Harith went back centuries, originating over disputed land territory. The animosity and bitterness on both sides was now so ingrained that its roots were all but forgotten. The shifting sands of time had done nothing to smooth over the differences between the two nations; in fact with each generation it seemed the wall of resentment grew ever higher.

Which made this debacle surrounding Azeed all the more dangerous. Zayed knew that his first momentous job as the newly crowned sheikh had to be to negotiate a peace initiative before the absurd threat of war that was rumbling between the two countries was allowed to take hold. Only then could he begin to tackle the other inherent problems.

Taking a deep slug of the burning whisky, he slammed

the glass back down on the sideboard and rolled back his shoulders to ease the tension. *If my friends could see me now.* Zayed let out a low snort of derision. He imagined meeting up with Stefan, Rocco and Christian in some swanky bar somewhere and regaling them with the story of what had happened this evening. The Columbia Four, he and his three trusty comrades were so named because they had met at Columbia University, shared their larger than life experiences whenever they got together, each one more than living up to the youthful motto they had adopted: *memento vivere*, remember to live. This year was certainly proving to be a momentous year for all of them, all three of his friends having married in quick succession, the last wedding, Stefan's, having taken place just a month ago.

Now, as the last remaining bachelor, it was up to Zayed to provide the outrageous entertainment. And he could make a good story of tonight. The lilac-eyed beauty huddled in his bed, him leaping on top of her, pinning her down, nothing but a skimpy towel around his waist to protect his modesty. He could imagine them roaring with laughter, slapping him on the back, ordering another round of drinks from one of the elegant hostesses to toast his hilarious escapade.

Except that Zayed didn't feel like laughing, and he certainly didn't feel like celebrating. Something about the look in Nadia's dazzling eyes as she had been escorted from the room by a servant niggled at him, haunted him. He still had no idea what she was doing here. What would make a young woman like that do something so debasing, so extreme, so downright dangerous? Reaching thoughtfully for his glass, Zayed raised it to his lips. Despite her provocative behaviour, the more Zayed thought about her, the more sure he was that she was not at all what she appeared to be. The haughty tilt of her chin, the imperious way she had spoken to him, the delicate, pale-skinned hands that looked as if they had never seen a day's toil in their life, all added up to a very different creature from the one who had virtually prostituted herself in his bed.

Tomorrow he would find out. And with a jolt of surprise he realised he was already looking forward to it. Infuriating she might be, but this Nadia was also a very beautiful, intriguing, not to mention sexy young woman. Something the very male part of him was refusing to ignore.

# CHAPTER THREE

NADIA AWOKE THE next morning against the sumptuous pillows of her gilded four-poster bed. But with a flash of realisation she remembered where she was, not in the straitjacketed safety of her bedroom in the palace of Harith, but somewhere deep within the walls of the sworn enemy of her kingdom, the palace of Gazbiyaa.

But not for much longer. Presumably she would shortly be escorted to the gates and told to disappear. She didn't know where to, or even how, but she had to accept that her mission here had failed. Her attempt to seduce Sheikh Zayed, to persuade him to take her virginity and then marry her out of honour, had failed miserably. Far from building the framework to try to find peace between their two nations, all she had done was antagonise the man she was trying to seduce and humiliate herself into the bargain.

And as for her family… Was there any possibility that she could return home and keep from them what she had done? Come up with some plausible story for her absence?

For that was her only hope now, all she could cling to. Because one thing was for sure: if her father and brother ever found out that she had even visited the kingdom of Gazbiyaa, let alone prostituted herself in the sheikh's bed, she would be dead to them now. And that was in the literal use of the word.

Some clothes had been mysteriously laid out for her:

a demure outfit of a knee-length skirt and a cream silk blouse. Hardly what she would have chosen, but certainly a darned sight better than yesterday's costume, whose gems still winked at her from the corner of the room where she had hurled it last night. She was just getting dressed when there was a tap on the door and a servant entered.

'I come with a message from His Royal Highness.' The servant's eyes were respectfully cast down. 'His Highness wishes to speak with you. I am to accompany you to his quarters.'

Nadia hesitated. To be honest she had assumed that she would be the last person he would want to see. By the look of disgust on his face last night it had appeared that if he never saw her again it would be too soon, and only the fear of her being raped or murdered on the night streets of Gazbiyaa had prevented him from having her evicted from the palace there and then. But then, the feeling was mutual. Having to face the handsome sheikh in the cold light of day after the way she had behaved was more than she could bear. No, this was a new day and there was no reason why she should have to take orders from him.

'Please inform His Royal Highness that I have made other plans.' As if to demonstrate those plans, as much to herself as to the elderly servant, she straightened her skirt and arranged the collar of her blouse. 'I'm afraid a meeting this morning will not be possible.'

The servant shifted uncomfortably. 'His Royal Highness is expecting me to accompany you now.'

Nadia felt herself bristle with indignation. While she had no desire to get this servant into trouble, at little more than five feet tall and old enough to be her grandmother, she hardly looked as if she was going to be able to force Nadia to go against her will. But just as this thought was taking hold two burly guards appeared from nowhere, flanking the servant, the rippling muscles of their folded arms providing all the proof she needed that, actually, she probably would do as she was told.

Zayed was sitting at the far end of a vast conference table when Nadia was borne forward in her bodyguard sandwich. She scowled as she found herself sinking into a chair opposite him.

'Good morning.' He dismissed the guards with a curt wave of his hand. 'I trust you slept well?'

Nadia's scowl deepened. As if he would care how well she slept. She had no intention of swapping false pleasantries with him. 'Perhaps you would like to tell me what I am doing here.' She tossed back her head.

'Interesting.' Sitting very upright now, Zayed fixed her with a piercing stare. 'I had rather assumed it was going to be *you* telling *me* what you are doing here.'

Nadia shifted on the leather seat beneath her, all hope that she might have been allowed to just disappear and not face the embarrassing inquest into last night's behaviour now fading fast. She let her eyes quickly scan the man at the far end of the table. Darkly, dangerously handsome, he still exuded the same confident authority as before, only now a calm determination replaced yesterday's more heated manner. And a crisp white shirt concealed the broad expanse of muscled chest. 'I can't see that it matters now.'

'It may not matter to you, but I am not accustomed to finding strange young women hiding in my bed. Perhaps you will at least indulge my curiosity.'

It didn't look as if she had much choice. Zayed's voice might be softly coaxing, but the steely sarcasm beneath was all too clear.

'Okay, fine.' Taking a deep breath, Nadia straightened her shoulders and tipped her chin. She could tell him part of her story, at least. Hopefully that would be enough to satisfy his irritating curiosity and she could get away from here. 'I came here to escape an arranged marriage.'

'An arranged marriage?'

'Yes.' She took another breath. She really didn't want to go into this. 'My father has arranged a marriage for me, but I don't want to marry him so I decided to run away.' She shrugged her shoulders in a 'that's all there is to it' sort of way.

At least this part of her story was true. Her father *had* arranged a marriage for her. After she had stubbornly refused the string of suitors that had been paraded before her over the past few years, he had finally lost all patience and announced the choice had been made for her; she was to be the second wife of the sheikh of a neighbouring kingdom, a man nearly thirty years her senior, and she was indeed fortunate this sheikh was prepared to take her on, considering her advanced age, all twenty-eight years of it, and her reputation for speaking her mind.

It was at this point that desperation had turned to a wild recklessness and Nadia had known that she had to seize the chance to do something with her life before it was too late. And to do that she had to use the only weapon she had in her armoury: her virgin body. A plan had formed in her head. If she had to marry, then she was going to make it count. She would use her marriage to heal the divide between Harith and Gazbiyaa and try to prevent war.

'Forgive me if I am being stupid here—' Zayed's eagle-eyed stare showed him to be anything but '—but if this is true, I fail to understand why escaping an arranged marriage necessitates creeping into my bed and offering yourself up to me.'

Nadia fiddled with the pearl button on her cuff. He was obviously quite determined to pursue this. 'Because if you had…if we had…then we would have had to marry and then I couldn't be forced into marrying anyone else.'

'Whoa!' His derisory laugh cut right through her. 'Aren't you getting a little ahead of yourself here?' He leaned back, relaxed now, as if beginning to enjoy himself. 'At the risk of appearing ungallant, why would you assume that one night of passion with you would be enough to convince me that I should marry you on the spot? You obviously rate your attributes very highly.'

Nadia lowered her eyes. 'Because I would have given you my honour. And surely that is the most precious gift of all?'

Zayed frowned at her. Well, that had told him. Suddenly he felt as if he were the one in the wrong here. By not taking her up on her offer he had scuppered her plans and besmirched her character at the same time. How had that happened? He looked down the length of the table to where Nadia sat, her mirror image reflected in the polished wooden surface, like a playing-card queen. Sitting very upright, her head held high, the thick weight of black curls pushed back over her shoulders, she looked both imperious and vulnerable. And still remarkably sexy, despite the conservative outfit that so primly covered the tempting body he knew was underneath. He cleared his throat.

'So let me get this straight. You flee from an arranged marriage to the bed of a total stranger with the idea of getting him to marry you instead. How, exactly, does that work?'

'My future husband would have been a total stranger. At least this way I would have been the one making the decision. I would have been exerting my own free will, had some say in who I would marry.'

'Even if your choice of future husband didn't.'

He saw Nadia's faint flinch as his barb hit its target but she recovered herself almost immediately, that chin tipped high, her full lips tightly closed as if she didn't intend to dignify his remark with an answer.

'And this man? The one you don't want to marry. Who is he? What's so bad about him?'

'Everything.'

'Presumably your family don't think so?'

'They see it as an advantageous match. That's all they care about. Plus they just want to see me married off so I don't cause them any more trouble.'

'You, a troublemaker? Who would have thought it?'

The serious flash in Nadia's lilac eyes withered his lighthearted comment. This was obviously no laughing matter. 'I simply have opinions, a mind of my own. As a woman that is not considered acceptable. Something you wouldn't understand.'

But Zayed did understand. His own mother, Latifa Al Afzal, had waited until the very last moment to have her say. But what she had revealed and the way she had chosen to reveal it had rocked the very foundations of the kingdom of Gazbiyaa. And irrevocably altered the path of Zayed's life.

Secretly securing an interview on one of the state-controlled Gazbiyaan television channels, Sheikha Latifa Al Afzal had started by telling the stunned audience that she was suffering from terminal cancer. In a weak but steady voice she had explained that she was quite ready to meet her fate, but first she had an important announcement for the people of her kingdom.

In keeping with the tradition of the laws of the land, her husband's reign as sheikh was shortly coming to an end. But he was to be succeeded not by his elder son, Azeed Al Afzal, but by the couple's younger son, Zayed. For Azeed was not, in fact, her biological son, but the child of a woman with whom her husband had had a brief relationship. This woman had died giving birth to him and, even though Latifa had raised Azeed as her own, loved Azeed as her own, there was one vital fact that could not be kept secret any longer. His birth mother had come from Harith. Azeed was half Harithian.

The fallout from this disclosure had been truly terrible. Zayed's father had exploded with fury that his wife had exposed the secret of Azeed's parentage, especially in such a public way, but the news of her illness and his genuine despair that she was dying had diverted his rage to his sons, to his kingdom, to the world in general.

The kingdom of Gazbiyaa had been thrown into turmoil, shocked to the core that Prince Azeed, whom they had seen as their future ruler, shared his blood with their greatest enemy. Zayed's father appeared to be dangerously close to losing control, and rioting in the streets was only prevented because his term of office was about to expire.

Azeed, meanwhile, had simply disappeared, storming out without a word to anyone. The shock of the news had presumably been so utterly devastating that he couldn't bear to stay in the palace a moment longer. Which meant that all eyes had turned to the second son. Zayed, the playboy prince.

Three years younger than his brother, Zayed had led an untroubled and privileged life, educated first at Eton College in England, then at Columbia University, New York. In truth he had barely given a thought to his own country, far too absorbed with the buzz of expanding his business empire and distraction of his friends and the many beautiful women who crossed his path. Gazbiyaa had seemed a long way away, his brother's inheritance his brother's responsibility.

But his mother's extraordinary declaration had changed *everything*.

Immediately leaving New York and the life he had made for himself there, Zayed had arrived at his mother's bedside just in time to take her frail hand and listen to her halting explanation. With heartbreaking humility she

had apologised for deceiving him, explaining that she had
wanted him to grow up without the burden of the future
blighting his early life. That even though she had always
known that she would have to reveal that he, Zayed, must
be crowned the next sheikh of Gazbiyaa, both because of
his birthright but more important for the stability of the
kingdom, she hoped he had enjoyed the freedom she had
gifted him until now.

With her voice fading to little more than a whisper,
Zayed had leaned in closer as his mother had begged him
to talk to Azeed, to explain to him why she had had to do
what she had done. For not only was Azeed temperamen-
tally unsuited to the role of sheikh, but if he continued
to threaten war against Harith he would inadvertently be
inciting a conflict against a country whose blood ran in
his veins.

As the last threads of life had slipped through his mother's fingers, Zayed had promised to make her peace with
Azeed, and she had allowed herself to slip into the oblivion of death, her voice finally heard.

Now Zayed stared at the spirited young woman before
him. So very much alive, so vibrant; he could sense her
determination, the strength of her will. He could see the
way she was fighting to take control of her own destiny
right now, to avoid the shadowy half-life his own mother
had accepted. There was no way she was going to leave it
until her deathbed to make her mark on this world.

And he admired Nadia for it. It showed guts, all right,
and that, combined with her undoubted beauty, was a fascinating combination. A crazy idea was suddenly beginning to take hold. He forced himself to put the brakes on it.

'So should I be flattered that this free will of yours has
brought you to my door?' He tipped back his head. 'Or
should I say my bed?'

Nadia wrinkled her small nose distastefully, as if by

reminding her of her actions he was degrading himself.
He had no idea how she did that.

'You were certainly a better proposition.'

'Well, that's something, I suppose. In what way?'

'I have only seen one photograph of my intended, but
it showed him to be old and fat and bald.'

'Right.' Laughing now, Zayed leaned back and crossed
one long leg over the other at the knee, gripping his ankle.
'Careful, Nadia. You don't want me to be getting big-
headed.'

'I suspect I am too late for that.'

Another swipe. Like a cat's paw, haughty and elegant,
but ultimately futile. Even though Zayed knew he could
close her down in a second he still had to remind himself who was playing with whom here. He was surprised
to find he was enjoying himself. Something about being
around Nadia lifted his spirits, and there hadn't been much
to do that lately.

He had already been subjected to another of his father's
rants this morning. Apparently the palace was alive with
gossip that the new sheikh had been discovered wrestling
on the bed with an unknown beauty last night. With his
playboy image preceding him, this was all the fodder they
needed to confirm their suspicions that Sheikh Zayed was
nothing more than a serial philanderer. That, unlike his
brother Azeed, he would never be a strong ruler. That the
kingdom of Gazbiyaa was going to descend into some
kind of mire of debauched hedonism if this *Westernised*
sheikh had his way.

Zayed hadn't bothered to try to explain his innocence.
Or point out that his father was hardly blame-free when it
came to his relationships with women, bearing in mind the
situation they were now in. He hadn't even suggested that
maybe the servants should learn to be more discreet. There
was no point. He had already learned that in Gazbiyaa a

problem had to be circumnavigated in order to be successfully addressed. And that was why this crazy idea refused to go away.

'Well, much as I would like to believe that it was my dashing good looks that drew you to me, I can't help wondering if the fact that I am the sheikh of an extremely wealthy kingdom may have had some bearing on your decision.'

'I have no interest in your wealth.' There it was again, that aloof disregard. But he believed her. He had come across a few gold-diggers in his time; in fact he prided himself that he could spot them a mile off. And even though he'd had to ask, he had already known that, for Nadia, this wasn't about money. 'Now, if you have quite finished with the insulting remarks, may I be allowed to leave?'

She started to stand, scraping back her chair, but at his end of the table Zayed rose faster than her and his movement halted hers.

'No, wait. Sit down.' He leaned forward, his arms locked on the table in front of him. Suddenly he realised he didn't want her to go. Not yet. Not at all. 'We haven't finished our conversation yet.'

'I believe we have.' Nadia gave him a barely audible sniff, but did sit back down in her seat.

'I may have a proposition to put to you.'

'What sort of proposition?' She crossed one leg over the other and, lacing her fingers, rested her chin lightly on them as she coolly surveyed him. Zayed was struck again by her astonishing poise.

'Well, as I understand it, you came here with the intention of persuading me to marry you. It might surprise you to know that I am considering the idea.'

He paused, scanning her face for the expected surprise, astonishment even. But it wasn't there. Just the calm, composed regard. She arched perfectly shaped eyebrows to indicate that he should continue.

'As I am the sheikh of Gazbiyaa you will understand that it is expected that I should take a wife.'

'Of course.'

'And in my case, probably the sooner the better.' He gave a small frown, acutely aware that Nadia was analysing every word, watching every movement of his facial muscles. 'There are certain misconceptions about me, rumours about my past. I need to dispel them. I believe a swift marriage would do that.'

'I see.' Her clipped replies were beginning to get on his nerves. It was starting to feel as if he was in the dock and she was waiting for his testimony. Well, she wasn't getting one. His past was his business and he certainly didn't have to justify it to her. He hardened his voice.

'Securing stability for the kingdom is of paramount importance right now. These are difficult times. I have to show the people that they can put their faith in me, that I am totally committed to the role of sheikh and can be trusted to rule this country skilfully and fairly. I will do anything within my power to achieve this.'

'And that includes getting married?'

'Yes.'

'To me?'

'Yes. Theoretically.' He could hardly believe he was saying this.

'So you are saying that as your wife I would be helping you to bring peace and stability to Gazbiyaa?'

'Well, indirectly, yes, I suppose I am.'

Finally the icy reserve had cracked and the glow of excitement that shone through the widening fissure seemed to light her from within, highlighting her body, gently flushing her pale cheeks and dancing in her eyes. God, she was beautiful.

Though the fact that it was only the idea of being able to do something to help the kingdom that had produced this alchemic change rather than any pretence that he himself might be quite a catch wasn't lost on him. In fact he was annoyed to feel a physical kick to his pride. He wasn't used to such indifference from members of the opposite sex.

'And I would be treated as your equal? Have my opinions listened to?'

'I don't imagine for one moment that I would be able to stop you.' Wasn't that the truth? He dimly registered that she was cross-examining him again when it should have been the other way round. But her enthusiasm was infectious, seductive. Downright sexy. Something, a gut reaction perhaps, told him that this could work.

And he was used to trusting his gut instinct. It rarely let him down in business, helping him to secure the lucrative deals that his competitors wouldn't touch and, equally important, steering him away from the disasters that looked so tempting on paper.

Could this be described as a business deal? If so it was certainly an unusual one. But if he was being honest, it wasn't so much his gut that was making this decision as another, lower part of his anatomy. He shifted in his seat.

'The way I see it, a marriage between the two us could prove to be mutually beneficial. I would be saving you from an unsavoury union and, in return, you would be helping me to restore the confidence of the people of Gazbiyaa. Showing them that they can put their trust in me, that I am an honourable man. Call it a contract between us, if you like.'

'A contract?'

'Yes. A wedding contract.'

He watched as Nadia assimilated this information, the elegant sweep of her neck as she turned slightly to one side to think, her concentration showing in the way she nipped one side of her full bottom lip with small white teeth.

The room was quiet apart from the low tick of a clock somewhere in the shadows and the faint hum of the air conditioning.

Finally she turned back to face him, her direct gaze meeting his full on.

'In that case I accept your proposal.' Her wide eyes held his with their unblinking clarity. 'I will agree to marry you.'

# CHAPTER FOUR

'WE ARE FINISHED, miss.' Finally satisfied, the leader of the fluttering team of female attendants stood back so that they could all admire their handiwork.

There was an expectant pause as they waited for her to turn and look at her reflection in the enormous, gilt-framed mirror behind her, but Nadia hesitated, needing a second to hold back the nerves that were clawing at her throat. She knew that once she actually saw herself, bedecked and bejewelled in preparation for the ceremony, there would be no hiding from the fact that this was actually going to happen. She was about to marry Sheikh Zayed Al Afzal.

It had all been arranged with such dizzying speed. No sooner had she agreed to Zayed's wedding contract than she had found herself being led down a series of echoing corridors to break the joyous news to his father. Except of course it wasn't joyous news; it was a purely practical arrangement. The very use of the word *contract* had made that perfectly clear and she hated it. But she was hardly in a position to be demanding hearts and flowers, no matter how much, privately, she might have loved them. After all, she was the one with the guilty secret, the one who was so deviously deceiving him. After the wedding she was going to have to confess to him who she really was—none other than Princess Nadia of Harith. And the very thought of that made the heavy knot of anxiety in her stomach start to unfurl and twist around inside her like a venomous snake.

So far no one had suspected anything. Zayed's father, Ghalib Al Afzal, had asked no questions of her when Zayed had presented her to him as his intended wife. In fact he had barely looked at her, giving her no more than a cold, cursory glance before nodding briefly at his son to acknowledge that he was at last doing something to address his flawed image. But for all his surly rudeness Nadia saw an old man obviously grieving the loss of his wife.

For his part, Zayed had just assumed that she was from Gazbiyaa and Nadia had tacitly kept it that way. She was helped by the fact that few people in the wider world knew she existed, let alone what she looked like. Her father had kept her hidden away, like a valuable possession to be used for bartering purposes only, to be sold for the most advantageous gain. At the time she had hated it, riled against it, despising the way she was treated and infuriating her father by turning down his choice of suitors. But now her anonymity worked in her favour.

At Nadia's insistence, the wedding invitations had been kept deliberately vague. With so many other things occupying his time, crowding his head, Zayed had taken her adamant statement that she didn't want her family to know of their marriage at face value, assuming that she knew best and never for one moment suspecting the real reason.

She had seen very little of him in the few short weeks since their marriage had been decided upon. His duties as sheikh of this powerful kingdom seemed onerous and never ending, and it was rare for him to have any time to himself, and even rarer for him to spend it with her. If she felt that she was just another of the projects that he was managing, that was because she was.

A rustle beside her reminded her that several pairs of eyes were watching her, eagerly waiting for her reaction to all their hard work. Taking in a steadying breath, Nadia slowly turned to look at her reflection.

She let out a gasp. Never had she imagined that she could look so beautiful. Her dress fitted her perfectly. Sweeping over one shoulder, it left the other bare as the fitted bodice held her breasts high and emphasised her tiny waist. The metres of silk that made up the skirt and the veil that was pinned to the back of her head were as fine as a dragonfly's wings and shimmered gently as she turned to look at herself, pooling at her feet when she stopped. A pale, watery green, the colour of a limestone rock pool, the whole garment was hand-embroidered with gold and platinum thread and decorated with thousands of crystals and seed pearls in an intricate, delicate pattern that swept diagonally down the bodice, then scattered randomly across the skirt. The effect was sophisticated and ethereal and utterly breathtaking.

Closer inspection showed that no part of her body had been spared attention or adornment by this group of women. From her delicately hennaed feet that had been eased into golden jewel-encrusted sandals to the stunning collection of antique jewellery, heavy with diamonds and pearls, that had been fastened around her neck, dangled from her ear lobes and somehow swept up into her hair so that the largest teardrop pearl hung perfectly down the centre of her forehead.

'Thank you.' She spoke to the collective reflections of the attendants, her long silence now beginning to show as concern on their faces. 'Thank you very much.' She would have liked to have said more but didn't trust herself. Her emotions were already dangerously unstable and she suspected that to open up, even to praise these kindly women for all their hard work, might tip her over the edge.

She sucked in another deep breath. She had to be strong. Today was her wedding day. And what a wedding it was to be.

If Nadia had thought it might be a small affair, with the

time scale being so short and the unconventional agreement she and Zayed had reached, she couldn't have been more wrong. Her prospective father-in-law obviously saw the occasion as a chance to prove to the world the extreme wealth and prosperity of the kingdom of Gazbiyaa, and that meant a celebration the like of which the kingdom had never seen before.

Nadia had wandered around in dazed astonishment at the transformation of the palace into a sumptuous wedding venue. The interconnected staterooms had been opened up and now row upon row of white chairs were positioned in readiness for the ceremony. And on a raised dais at the far end, two gilded thrones were waiting for the bride and groom. Just the sight of them had sent a ripple of alarm through Nadia, that it was actually her that would be sitting on that throne. That this was really happening.

Every room in the palace had been bedecked with exotic flowers, the rarest, most beautiful blooms, flown in from around the world and tended to by a team of florists who had teased them into life-size shapes of peacocks and elephants or gathered them into enormous arrangements and suspended them from the ceilings.

Outside, acres of garden had been transformed into a Bedouin fantasy, with soaring, tented structures, the interiors dressed with the finest, most colourful silks draped and swathed in voluminous abundance, and priceless Persian rugs scattered underfoot. Here the seating was arranged for the entertainment, with comfortable armchairs and enormous cushions positioned for the most advantageous view.

Nadia had seen some of the entertainers arriving, troupes of jugglers, acrobats and stilt walkers. She had even watched the fire-eaters practising from her bedroom window, lighting up the night sky with their extraordinary dangerous-looking feats. She knew there were to be animal processions, too, elephants as well as camels, and even a rumour that a poor tiger had been flown in and was caged somewhere on the premises, a reluctant guest at the wedding.

Well, that would make two of them. Three, in fact, if you counted Zayed. For in no way did the exuberant wedding preparations reflect the feelings of the bride and groom. As far as Nadia was concerned it was a means to an end, something that had to be got through as best she could to try to secure her kingdom's future. If it meant partaking in this ridiculous charade, then she would do it. If it meant sharing a bed with Sheikh Zayed she would do that, too. For sacrifices had to be made for the greater good.

Although the thought of going to bed with Zayed was not a sacrifice. Far from it. Alone at night she had found herself becoming increasingly obsessed with the idea of what it would be like. The thought of Zayed, in all his naked, muscular glory, taking her in his arms, covering her body with his own, not in anger like last time but ready to make love to her, to take away her virginity, filled her with such a heated desire that it made her body writhe and undulate beneath the cool sheets, her hand even tentatively straying between her legs in an attempt to ease this ache. It shocked her, this totally unfamiliar feeling, this pulsing, burning, hot-blooded sexual awakening that just the thought of Zayed alone could produce. And it frightened her, too. Because with it came a loss of control, over her own body and over her feelings for Zayed. And that was something she could never let happen.

'You look charming, Nadia.' Two female elders of the Al Afzal family had swept into the room, and Nadia's attendants silently disappeared. Leaning forward, one of them carefully lifted the veil so that it now covered Nadia's face. 'There. Now you are ready.'

\* \* \*

Nadia nodded, quite unable to speak. In accordance with tradition, these extravagantly dressed women were here to escort her to the nikah, the wedding ceremony, and even though they weren't unkind, they most certainly weren't her own mother, who had no idea that her only daughter was getting married today.

In a daze of unreality she felt herself being borne along to meet her groom. The trio entered the stateroom through a door that led directly to the steps up to the dais, as, on the other side of the room, Zayed did the same.

Nadia climbed the steps with a thudding heart, aware of, but definitely not looking at, the vast number of guests that she knew were watching her. A reverential hush had spread over the room.

They reached their twin thrones at exactly the same time and stopped, facing one another. And the sight of her husband-to-be managed to steal away the last bit of breath from Nadia's constricted chest. For never had she seen such an utterly, devastatingly handsome man. He was dressed in an oyster-coloured sherwani, the heavy brocade fabric of the fitted knee-length coat embroidered with white and gold silks and the high collar and cuffs encrusted with pearls. Five gold and pearl buttons were fastened down the front. He stood tall and proud and darkly magnificent, and Nadia could only hope that her veil hid the flush of heated longing that the sight of him had produced.

They stared at each other, and for a brief second it was just the two of them, coming together to embark upon this crazy adventure. Zayed's eyes flitted down the length of Nadia's body and when he raised them again, silently mouthing the word *wow*, Nadia felt a ridiculous sweep of pride. Then he gently took her hand in his and they both lowered themselves onto their respective thrones.

And so the short ceremony began. With the sonorous

voice of the imam reading from the Koran beside them, Nadia risked raising her eyes to take in the sea of people before her. There were so many guests, hundreds of them; royalty and heads of state, prime ministers and foreign dignitaries, flown in from all four corners of the world to witness the marriage of Sheikh Zayed Al Afzal. And also to witness the enormous wealth and mighty power of the kingdom of Gazbiyaa. Something that Zayed's father, who was imperiously watching the ceremony from his front-row seat, was determined that this wedding would showcase.

'Nadia Ayesha. Do you accept Zayed Omar Jamal as your husband and life partner?'

Startled, Nadia realised that the imam was addressing her, that Zayed had already said his vows and now there were several hundred people waiting for her response. Pushing the words past a throat as dry as the desert sands, she heard herself say, 'I accept Zayed Omar Jamal as my husband and life partner.'

She watched as Zayed slid the plain gold band onto her ring finger and held out his hand for her to do the same. Fighting to control the tremble of nerves, Nadia pushed it over his knuckle where it sat snugly against his dark skin, glinting at her malevolently.

'Then, I now declare you husband and wife.'

Zayed leaned towards her, and their eyes briefly met before he lifted her veil and planted the lightest of kisses against her mouth that was half-open in readiness.

She was sure she heard an 'aah' from somewhere in the crowd.

'How are you doing?'

Zayed looked down at his beautiful new bride as they stood beside the ridiculously towering wedding cake that was taller than she was. Nadia had behaved perfectly all afternoon, the very model of grace and decorum, a mixture of the perfect hostess and the demure newlywed; it was almost as if she had done this before. She had conversed with their guests, kissing, thanking and embracing an endless stream of people, smiling prettily or lowering her eyes modestly at their compliments and charming every single one of them. Just as she had charmed him. Although *charmed* wasn't really the right word in his case. *Seduced* might be a better one, or maybe just plain *got to*. Whatever it was, it was a surprising and powerful force.

But close to her now he could see the strain behind her eyes, and it was that that had prompted him to ask the question.

'Fine, thank you.' She tipped her chin in that particularly imperious way she seemed to reserve for him. 'I think it is all going very well.'

That hadn't been what he meant, and she knew it, but Zayed wasn't going to argue.

'Come on, then, let's see if we can slay this beast.' He gave the ceremonial sword in his hand a quick twirl before raising it to the lowest tier of the cake and waiting for Nadia to join him. He could feel the light tremble of her hand as it rested on top of his, and they set about pressing the blade into the cake.

The cutting of the cake meant that the banquet was finally over. One hundred different dishes prepared by the world's top chefs had been feasted upon, washed down with the finest of wines for those who chose to drink, and now it was time for the entertainment to commence.

The guests were starting to rise from the tables, easing their gastronomically sated bodies to standing and moving past the magnificent ice sculptures to the outside area where the band had already struck up, the strains of the Arabic beat throbbing in the background.

'Zayed, Nadia, over here!'

Across the room a handsome man had stood up and was wildly gesturing for them to come over and join his party. Nadia felt the warm pressure of Zayed's hand on the small of her back as he steered her through the maze of tables until he had reached them, and immediately the two other men at the table got to their feet. Their three beautiful wives were smiling broadly and gesturing to Nadia to join them, and with much kissing and backslapping and chair scraping they were all seated once more.

'Well, Zayed, who would have thought it? All four of us married!'

'Yes, Zayed, and I think you owe us an apology. It's only a few short weeks since mine and Clio's wedding and not a word then! In fact, wasn't there some talk about how you were going to have to party twice as hard to make up for the fact that we three were no longer on the market?'

'Stefan!' a striking redhead admonished her husband with a pointed stare. 'Please forgive my husband. I'm afraid when these four get together they revert to college roommates. It's just something we have to put up with.'

'Besides, I imagine when Zayed was making his boastful claims he hadn't met the beautiful Nadia.'

'Oi!' This time the admonishment came from Olivia as she pretended to glare at her husband.

'What?' Rocco gave a very Italian shrug of his shoulders. 'I'm just saying—'

'We know what you are just saying, thank you. Just be careful how you say it.' Her eyes twinkled at him mischievously. 'Not that any of us are going to disagree with you. Nadia, you do look stunningly beautiful. I can't take my eyes off that dress.'

'Thank you.' Nadia smiled politely, but something inside hurt. She had been introduced to this lively group of people the night before, Zayed's three closest friends and their wives. From the grin on his face she could see that

Zayed was taking a few moments to relax, be himself, be happy. These people represented his previous life, the one he'd had to leave behind when he'd been forced to return to Gazbiyaa. Forced to marry her.

'So tell me, who is the designer?'

'Look at this, she tells me off and now Liv wants to talk shop!' Rocco leaned back with his arms behind his head and grinned at the table.

'This is not talking shop. Well, maybe it is a bit.' Olivia laughed and touched her blond hair. 'Sorry—' she smiled her explanation '—my husband and I are in the fashion business and you never quite switch off. And Alessandra here is a fashion photographer. She and I have been trying to hazard a guess as to who the designer could be, though now I can see it close up I don't think we have any idea. The detail on the stitching is amazing. Look, Alessandra.'

Alessandra pushed her chair back, needing to make room for the growing baby bump before she could lean in for a closer look.

'So, Zayed.' Christian dragged his adoring eyes away from his wife and cocked his head on one side. 'This wedding was very sudden. There isn't something you want to tell us, is there?'

'Christian!' Alessandra mock glared at her husband before taking hold of Nadia's hand. 'So please, Nadia, put us out of our misery. Who did make this exquisite masterpiece?'

'Um...' Nadia looked down at her hand resting in Alessandra's, then raised her eyes to the expectant faces of these lovely women. The fact was she had no idea. It hadn't seemed to matter up until now. She'd had bigger things to worry about than who had made her dress. But suddenly it seemed to matter an awful lot. She so wanted to belong, be part of this happy group.

The men had moved on to another conversation; she

could hear Rocco asking Zayed about his brother, whether he was here at the wedding, and Zayed briskly replying that he had declined his invitation.

'I'm sorry,' Nadia faltered, distracted by Zayed and upset that she didn't know the answer. 'I don't recall the name. Stupid of me.' Even more stupid was the hard knot of hurt that she tried to swallow back down her throat, the burn of tears behind her violet eyes.

'Well, whoever it is, they have done a fantastic job.' Pushing back her chair, Clio went to stand up. 'D'you know what? I think I need to freshen up.' She pointedly raised her eyebrows at her friends. 'Would you be so kind as to show me the way to the ladies' room, Nadia? Even though I had a tour of this place last night, it's so vast that if I try to find it by myself you may never see me again.'

'I will come, as well.' Alessandra got to her feet, spreading her hands across her tummy. 'Me and this little one never turn down a trip to the bathroom.'

Olivia rose, too, and soon their four faces were reflected in the ornate mirrors of the rest room.

'They are not wrong when they call this your big day, are they?' Clio was pulling a comb through her sleek red hair, but at the same time she was studying Nadia's face. 'You need to take a bit of time out, let your family and friends support you.'

It was meant as kindly advice, but when Nadia visibly stiffened the three perceptive women immediately noticed.

'I don't have any family here.' Defensiveness made her sound cold, unfriendly. And from the exchanged glances and almost imperceptible shrugs of the shoulders in the mirror, she could see their surprise. 'I am estranged from my family.'

'Oh. Well, we'll be your family now, won't we, girls?' Deliberately overcheery, Olivia put an arm around her.

'You and Zayed are just perfect for one another, and I'm sure you are going to be so happy… Hey…what is it?'

As the tears started to roll down Nadia's cheeks Olivia pulled her to her chest, closely followed by Clio and Alessandra. 'Come on now, a group hug. I know what it's like—your emotions are all over the place, aren't they?—but you are doing a great job and Zayed is a good man. You've made the right choice, you know.'

'Do you think so?' Nadia snuffled from under the middle of the scrum.

'We know so. Just ask the hundreds of other women who have tried and failed to get his ring on their finger!'

'But seriously, Nadia.' Clio's cut-glass English accent was quietly authoritative. 'I know Zayed well. We were at university together, and he gave me away at my wedding, supported me when I needed him most. You won't find a better man.'

There was a telling pause, eventually broken by Olivia. 'And you're not on your own, you know. You can count on us now. We four have to stick together. We need all the solidarity we can get to put up with those alpha husbands of ours.'

'Too true,' Alessandra agreed. 'The trick is to make them think they are getting their own way when really they are doing what we want all along. There's a knack to it, but we can help you.'

'Thanks!' Coming up for air, Nadia found herself smiling, and as the arms around her loosened she reached for the box of tissues that Olivia was holding out. 'Thank you so much. I'm feeling better now. It all just got on top of me a bit.'

'That's the good bit, still to come.'

'Liv!'

'What? I'm just saying. Enjoy it, Nadia. Your wedding night is special. Make the most of it. Our four husbands may all suffer from the belief that they are God's gift to the female race but Zayed is a very lucky man to have you. Make sure he knows it.'

'Okay, thank you for the advice. And for the support too, it means a lot.' With a determined sniff Nadia leaned forward towards the mirror, then recoiled in dismay. 'Oh, no. I look a mess.'

'Nonsense. You look annoyingly beautiful, if a little smudged. But that's nothing that a couple of minutes in the hands of experts like us can't repair. Come on, girls, out with your make-up bags.'

Their husbands had left the banqueting room by the time the quartet returned, so, arms linked, the women made their way outside to join the noisy throng. A group of young men were cheering loudly and in unison, and as they drew closer it became apparent why. Watched at a safe distance by the assembled guests, Zayed was being tossed, high into the air, arms and legs flailing, his sherwani coat flapping open. And at the centre of this group of boisterous strength were the grinning faces and muscled arms of his greatest friends, Rocco, Christian and Stefan.

For the first time that day, Nadia found herself laughing. Especially when Olivia leaned towards her and whispered conspiratorially into her ear, 'We told you—they never grow up.'

As the evening wore on, Nadia started to relax, even beginning to enjoy herself. It was hard not to, given the scale of the lavish entertainment all around her, although she had looked away when it was the turn of the belly dancers to perform. She could do without that particular reminder of how she'd gotten here.

There were singers and drummers and lute players, weaving their way between the rainbow-coloured fountains, encouraging the guests up onto their feet to join in the dancing beneath the giant chandeliers that hung from the tented roof. Every now and then Nadia caught a glimpse of her new friends, pleased to see that they were obviously enjoying themselves.

More food was served, enormous platters of shish kebabs and tabbouleh, towering pyramids of baklava and *basbousa*, dried fruits and fresh.

Zayed, meanwhile, was being the perfect host, attentive, charming and solicitous, taking full advantage of the networking occasion that this undoubtedly was.

She would have expected nothing less of him, of course, but the way he worked the room with such practised ease somehow made her feel worse. He was playing a part, every bit as much as her, and for some reason that hurt. Every now and then he would appear beside her and she would be borne off to meet some foreign dignitary, or more specifically the foreign dignitary's wife, before he politely disappeared again, leaving her to watch from a distance as he embraced the flowing white robes of yet another VIP or leaned forward to better hear the words of another keffiyeh-covered head.

Finally the night of celebrations was drawing to a close. As the guests were encouraged to go outside for the fireworks display Nadia felt Zayed's arm snake deliciously around her waist as they led the way.

'So, wife, here we are.'

'Yes.' She was surprised to find she liked the term *wife*. And she definitely liked the way he was pulling her more closely to him, little darts of desire prickling her skin as she breathed in the citrus tang of his cologne, leaned into the span of his hand. 'Here we are.'

A series of bangs reverberated around them as a succession of silver and gold fireworks lit up the sky. They both tilted their heads to watch.

'I don't think I've told you yet how beautiful you look.'

'Thank you.' Nadia continued to gaze up at the sky,

the heat from Zayed's body pressing against her side and setting off a fireworks display all of its own inside her.

'No, I mean it. I couldn't have asked for a more beautiful bride. You have been amazing today, Nadia, and it can't have been easy. I want you to know how proud I am of you.'

Nadia felt her spine stiffen, the arm around her waist suddenly feeling controlling. She didn't want him to be proud of her, not like that. As Princess Nadia of Harith, being the perfect hostess had been the one skill she'd been expected to acquire. Look beautiful, behave with decorum and, most important, keep your opinions to yourself. It certainly wasn't something she wanted praise or recognition for.

'I'm sorry your family weren't here today though, that you didn't feel able to tell them about our marriage.'

Nadia froze, the fear that his casually delivered words might hold more meaning, that he had found out something about her today, holding her rigid.

She had had no contact with her family since she had left Harith, apart from getting one message to them to say that she was safe and well. They had no idea she was in Gazbiyaa and they certainly had no idea she had just married Sheikh Zayed Al Afzal. The excuse she had given Zayed, that she couldn't tell them because they would never forgive her for running away from her arranged marriage, was only the tip of an iceberg that would blot out the desert sun if her family knew the truth. Something they couldn't do until after the threat of war between the two kingdoms was over.

Surreptitiously, Nadia turned her head to try to read his face. His strong profile was still tipped back towards the sky, his face reflecting the glowing colours of the fireworks, but, feeling her eyes on him, he turned to look down at her. 'When things have settled down we'll find a way to some sort of reconciliation.'

There was no trace of sarcasm there or particular scrutiny. Just a desire to see her reconciled with her family.

And that only made her deceit feel a hundred times worse.

The last dramatic firework was drawing cheers from the crowd. The names *Nadia* and *Zayed* were emblazoned across the night sky, crackling and sparkling inside their golden heart. She heard Zayed laugh, and, pulling her closer to him again, he whispered against the top of her head, 'Our name in lights, Nadia. Who would have thought it?'

Who indeed? But as the last of the letters fizzled and died leaving nothing but a cloud of smoke, Nadia felt an icy shiver run through her. A splendid burst of celebration and then nothing. She just hoped it wasn't a portent for their marriage.

# CHAPTER FIVE

'WELL, I THINK we can safely say this is the bridal suite.' Closing the door behind them, Zayed stood and surveyed the scene, his jacket suspended by one finger over his shoulder. 'Either that or we've stepped into the middle of a wedding cake.'

Nadia could see what he meant. Before them stood an enormous oval-shaped bed that was raised on a platform studded with the heads of pink and cream roses, the perfect blooms arranged in careful rows as if they had been squeezed out of a giant piping bag. More rose petals were strewn around the bed and over the giant cushions around it, while above it metres of soft white fabric formed a canopy that swept up to the ceiling and was swathed in sumptuous folds to the sides of the room. A pair of giant floral arrangements on either side of the bed completed the extravagant scene.

Secretly Nadia thought it looked beautiful, so romantic, the perfect setting for the first night of passion between a couple in love. But that wasn't what they were, was it? This wasn't about love or heartfelt emotions, at least of the romantic kind. It was the love of their respective countries that had made them both enter into this *contract*, not a love for each other. Which somehow made the heady perfume of the roses seem strangely pungent.

'Someone has obviously gone to a lot of trouble.' She looked around her, nervously raising her hand to her throat.

'Better not waste it, then.' Stepping up onto the platform, Zayed tossed his jacket to one side and extended a hand to her. 'Welcome to my floral lair.'

Nadia felt herself being pulled up next to him, her heart thudding madly as she was pressed against his chest, which now, minus the jacket, was encased in a tight white cotton vest that moulded itself against the granite-hard planes of his torso like a second skin.

His arms wrapped around her back. With her head turned she could feel the beat of his heart, inhale his uniquely masculine scent, feel the sexual intensity pulsing between them like a physical force. Her whole body was filled with it, weakened by it. She realised that she wanted him. Badly.

Tentatively she raised her arms, slipping them under his and running them over his vest top, across the broad expanse of his shoulder blades and down to the narrowing of his waist, stopping at the waistband of his trousers. He felt so good, so completely male. Strong and athletic and yet twitching slightly beneath her fingers as they skittered over him. She loved that she had this small power over him, that despite his ever-present control, his rigid authority, she could do this to him. Loved, too, the growing evidence of her power that was now swelling beneath his trousers, pressing against her groin.

Angling back her head, Nadia closed her eyes and felt his breath sweep hot and dry across her cheeks. Sheer sexual excitement flooded through her, pumping the blood unnaturally fast through her veins, heating her core and plumping her lips that were desperately waiting for the kiss that had to come any minute now.

Except it didn't.

Instead, she felt Zayed pull back and as she warily opened her eyes she saw that he was staring down at her, his gaze narrowed, shuttered.

A flush crept up her throat, burning her cheeks, prickling her skin. Why was he looking at her like that? Humiliation lanced through her, his punishing stare scything through the tautness of her desire until her body sagged against his, her arms dropping by her sides.

She lowered her eyes to the bejewelled sandals on her feet, desperately trying to hide from Zayed the evidence of her body's betrayal. Hide behind the facade she had been struggling to keep up all day long.

But something about the quiet force of his eyes was threatening to finally steal the last bit of strength she had left. Playing the part of the perfect bride all day long had taken its toll and now, faced with this last challenge, she felt herself wobble, as if in the middle of a sagging tightrope.

Suddenly she felt very vulnerable, very alone. The enormity of what she had done, the crazy leap of faith she had taken to be here, was making the room begin to close in around her, a swell of panic rise in her chest. She was trapped in a loveless marriage to a man she hardly knew. A man who still knew nothing of who she really was. The fact that her whole body ached for him, craved his kiss, his touch, him to take her in a purely carnal way, only increased the hollowed-out sense of loneliness inside her. Because the strength of these feelings frightened her, she didn't know how to deal with them. And because she didn't know how she would cope if he rejected her now.

Forcing herself to breathe through the panic, Nadia struggled to find her balance. She couldn't teeter and fall now; it simply wasn't an option. This was all her own doing. She had made her bed, now she had to lie in it.

Although, as she raised her eyes again to Zayed's long stare, she suspected she could well be lying on that bed alone. Because far from returning the open, obvious desire that Nadia had naively revealed to him, he appeared to be regarding her more like some sort of mildly interesting social experiment. If she was desperate for him to throw her across this fairy-tale bed and make mad, passionate love to her, he was standing there like the epitome of controlled composure. Not to mention the epitome of every woman's fantasy. The bunched muscles of his bare arms were now crossed over his chest, the loose trousers slung low over his hips, a strip of olive skin dusted with dark hair visible between the tight white vest and the drawstring of his trousers.

Nadia swallowed hard. Well, she could be controlled, too. Rearing up, she took a step back, only to get her feet caught in the metres of fabric of her skirt and stumble against the edge of the platform.

'Careful.' Zayed's arms were immediately around her again, catching her before she fell, holding her steady against him. 'This bed arrangement should carry a health warning.'

Breathing over the top of Nadia's soft hair, Zayed realised it was Nadia herself who should carry the health warning. Being alone with her now was in danger of unravelling the last bit of self-control that he possessed. His whole body was screaming at him to give in, to claim her beautiful body, to do whatever he had to do to satisfy the lust that had been simmering inside him from the first moment he had laid eyes on her and now roared like a furnace.

But still he hesitated. He had to be sure that Nadia wanted this, too. And even though she had demonstrated her willingness just now, leaning into him, running her hands across his back in a delicate way that had jerked him to instant arousal, when he had pulled back to look into her eyes, what he had seen there had held him back. Desire yes, but mixed with anxiety. Passion, too, that seemed to have startled Nadia herself with its power and which could have so easily felled him there and then with its wide-eyed innocence. But it was a passion mixed with in-security, doubt. Zayed knew he had to try to slow things down, to do the right thing by Nadia, even if he was kill-ing himself in the process. Even if every second he held back from her was tightening the screws on his sensitised body like some sort of perverse, sadomasochistic torture.

Because something was obviously making Nadia ner-vous. Despite her poised exterior, her feisty attitude, the provocative behaviour of their first encounter, he had no doubt that she was sexually inexperienced. That she was a virgin, in fact. Was that why she seemed so tense?

Zayed couldn't remember the last time he'd had sex with a virgin. Probably ten years ago, back at Columbia Uni-versity. He and his friends, Christian, Stefan and Rocco, had had something of a reputation back then, one that was well deserved. No attractive woman had been safe from the predatory instincts and practised charm of these four young men with the world at their feet and the notches on their bedposts to prove it.

But this was different—completely different. Nadia was his wife; this relationship was permanent. He had to try to figure out what was going on in that beautiful head of hers before he could take it any further.

'Why don't we sit down?' Unfolding his arms, he took hold of her hand and led her the couple of steps to the edge of the bed, where he gently pulled her down beside him. 'So—' he turned so that he could see her face more clearly '—that was quite a day, wasn't it?'

'Yes.'

'I hope you haven't found it all too much of an ordeal.'

'No, of course not. It has been very enjoyable.' Her clipped tone somehow belied her words.

'But I'm sure you must be tired.'

'No, I'm fine.'

'Look, Nadia.' Turning over her hand in his, Zayed exposed the palm, as if the answer to the enigma that was Nadia could be read there. 'You can relax now, you know. Don't feel you have to keep up the pretence any longer.'

'What pretence?' Her hand had curled in his, a sharp edge to her voice. 'I don't know what you mean.'

'I mean—' Zayed lowered his voice, determined that she should understand him '—we don't have to do this now, you know.' He jerked his head back to indicate the petal-strewn elephant in the room behind them. 'It doesn't have to be tonight. If you are really not tired, perhaps I could get us some drinks sent up. We could just talk, get to know one another better. I would like to discover more about the real Nadia.' He raised his eyebrows, even risked a lopsided smile.

'There is nothing to discover.' Blocked again by her blunt reply, Zayed felt Nadia's petulance begin to grate through his patience. He sighed heavily.

'Then, maybe we should just go to our separate rooms.'

'Fine.' Snatching back her hand, Nadia used it to gather up her skirts, edging away from him. 'But if you don't want to make love to me, I would prefer it if you just came right out and said it.'

'For God's sake!' With a growl of exasperation Zayed leaped to his feet and turned to look down on Nadia. 'Of course I want to make love to you.' He raked a hand through his dark hair in pure frustration. 'Believe me, there is nothing I would like to do more.'

Wasn't it obvious? He was alone at last with the most hot, sexy, unconsciously erotic woman who he had ever met in his life. His fingers were itching to peel off that beautiful gown of hers and throw her across this ridiculous bed and devour her in the purely carnal way he craved. The way she was glaring at him now only intensified his lust; the jut of her chin, the slight flaring of those perfect nostrils, the thick black lashes lowered over eyes that looked as if they could slay him. Everything about her was pure torment. He cleared his throat, determined to give reason one last shot.

'But only if you want it, too.' He placed his hands firmly on his hips. 'What I am trying to say is, having sex with me tonight is not another duty you have to perform.'

There was a pause, the room perfectly quiet, the scent of the flowers filling the air. Then, purposefully rising to her feet, Nadia gave Zayed the full force of her jewel-bright eyes.

Slowly, deliberately, she crossed one hand over her chest and slid her finger under the single strap of her gown.

'Does this look like duty?'

With a physical jolt Zayed watched the strap fall down over the soft skin of her shoulder. The muscles in his throat contracted, his dark eyes dilating to ebony black.

'Or this?'

Now she was pulling down the side zip, her eyes fixed on his face, eyes heavy with seduction. Zayed forced down a gulp. The top of her dress had fallen to her waist, revealing a white boned corset that was both chaste and incredibly sexy at the same time. Her breasts were swelling over the top, her tiny waist held in tight.

'Perhaps you would like to help me out of the rest of it?' Nadia looked down at the sweep of her skirt, already squirming to ease the folds over her hips. 'I don't want to damage it.'

Zayed did. He wanted to rip it off her body with an urgency that scared him, to feast his eyes on what lay beneath with a desperation that he had never felt before. What was wrong with him? Forcing himself to find a modicum of self-control from somewhere, he reached towards her, realising with alarm that his hands were shaking with unadulterated lust. Never before had a woman had this effect on him.

Moving his hands to either side of her hips, he watched as the dress fell through his fingers to the ground, still telling himself that he could stop at any time. That he was simply helping his bride out of her wedding dress. But as he watched Nadia stepping out of the dress, bending to pick it up and drape it over the end of the bed, he knew he was lost, totally and utterly lost in the ruthless grip of sexual longing. From the bottom of the corset, suspenders stretched tight along her smooth thighs, holding up white silk stockings. She wore a pair of tiny white panties beneath. If there had ever been a point of no return, the sight of her now meant he had well and truly passed it; any resolve he might have had to resist her tonight was lost in the cloud of dust from his heels in his eagerness to grab her.

Almost in slow motion he raised his hands to her hair, loosening the clips that held it and watching as it fell in glorious disarray around her shoulders. He threaded his fingers through its silky richness, disentangling the jewellery that was nestling amongst the black curls before moving with an unsteady hand to undo her necklace and earrings.

There was the briefest of pauses as he stood to drink her in in all her erotic loveliness before he finally bent to kiss her lips, all rationality gone.

Slowly at first, he tested the plump fullness of her lips, then more firmly, touching and tasting, running his tongue tantalisingly between them as they opened to allow him to plunder the warm darkness inside, to feel, taste and explore, to feed the heady, shaky euphoria that was coursing through his veins like a drug, urging him on.

Like the tip of a crashing wave, he was up there and there was no going back, just the tremendous thrill of what was to come.

With her arms clasped around his neck, Nadia heard him moan into her mouth. This was the most incredible feeling she had ever experienced, all of her senses being ambushed at the same time. The touch of him, the taste, the heat, the spicy masculine smell, the scratch of his beard, all combined had taken over her brain completely, obliterating everything but the throbbing, yearning craving that pulsated where her body had once been.

Zayed moved to alter the angle of his head, then reclaimed her mouth, increasing the pressure as his hands ran over her bare shoulders, down the back of the corset and spread, warm and strong, over the cheeks of her scantily clad bottom. Now it was Nadia's turn to moan as she arched her back, pushing her groin towards him to invite his hands to caress her harder, to move to more intimate parts of her body. But the moan turned into a gasp as she felt his rock-hard arousal pressing against her abdomen, so big, so powerful that it had triggered a series of clenching spasms that threatened to knock her legs from under her. Clinging onto his neck for support now, she rose up on tiptoes, unconsciously trying to move his erection down lower, to feel it where she wanted it most.

'I want you so much.' She wasn't sure who said it, or even if the words had been spoken out loud, but with one swift movement Zayed was sweeping her off her feet and laying her firmly down on the bed.

He was tearing off his clothes with feverish speed. From her position, splayed across the middle of the bed, Nadia watched as he ripped off his vest and trousers, dimly wondering if she should be divesting herself of her undergarments in readiness for him. Finally the straining boxer shorts were flung to one side and he stood before her, gloriously naked.

Nadia stared. And then stared some more. She had already seen him virtually naked: the sculptured abs, the narrow waist, the coarse hair that arrowed down to his groin. She'd even felt his arousal pressed against her. And she had read about sex, had thought she had known what to expect. But nothing had prepared her for this, the sheer size of it, both the length and the girth… Was it possible that this could fit inside her? The idea both thrilled and astonished her.

Eventually she realised that Zayed hadn't moved, that he was watching her, watching him. She dragged her eyes up to his face.

'You have changed your mind?' He stood proudly, totally confident with his nakedness but doubt clawing his question.

'No.' Nadia pushed the word past her dry throat. 'No, it's not that.'

'You have never seen a man naked before?'

'No.' On safer ground now, Nadia confessed lightly, 'Not unless you count the movies.'

Zayed let out a strangled laugh. 'And in real life, it's not what you thought?'

'No. I don't know. It's just…'

'I'm not going to deny it, Nadia, I want you like crazy. But if you have changed your mind just say the word and—'

'No, I haven't changed my mind.' Braver now with more confirmation that he wanted her, Nadia pushed herself back against the pillows, squirming in unconscious invitation. 'I suppose I hadn't realised that it—you, I mean— would be so big.'

'Flattery, flattery.' Zayed's eyes twinkled with humour, but his voice had taken on the guttural growl of a man who needed release. With a couple of steps he was beside the bed, and then he was on top of her, his arms locked on either side of her head so that he could look down onto her face.

'I'll be as gentle as I can.' Slowly he lowered his body on top of her and claimed her lips again, the full length of his glorious body meeting hers all the way down, crushing her breasts beneath the corset, his erection pressing against her. Nadia felt the shuddering clenching of her internal muscles in response, the dampness between her legs.

'Perhaps we should get rid of these.' Parting their bodies enough to run one hand down to her hips, Zayed tugged at the scrap of lacy fabric and tossed her panties to the floor. Bringing his hand back up, he briefly traced the tingling bare flesh of one thigh beneath the suspenders before moving up to her moist folds, one expert finger teasing and rubbing a part of her that she hadn't even known existed and bringing about the most exquisite feeling of pleasure.

Already she could feel herself building to what she knew must be an orgasm, her first orgasm. With her nails digging into the hard flesh of Zayed's back she was about to moan, to quietly whimper and shudder her way over the edge of bliss when Zayed whispered softly into her ear, 'Not yet, baby, save it, save it for me.' Removing his finger, he replaced it with the throbbing tip of him, rubbing it firmly against her, sending Nadia soaring into spasms of ecstasy. Then, shifting his position, he started to push into her, slowly at first, testing the way, hot and firm but gentle, too. But finding her wetness as confirmation he let out a low groan and started to sink his length into her, farther and deeper and deeper.

Nadia gasped, her nails digging so hard into his back that she had to be drawing blood, clinging on to him for dear life as the extraordinary feeling consumed her.

'Nadia?' His voice was dry, husky, as if coming from a long way away.

'Yes!' She could barely speak, so her body spoke for her as she tipped her pelvis forward to drive him in that final bit, producing another guttural groan.

'God, Nadia, you feel so good.' He had started to move

now, rhythmically thrusting inside her, each forward motion more powerful than the last, more intense, more piercingly pleasurable and excruciatingly overwhelming than the one before. 'I don't think I can hang on much longer...'

As his words tailed off Nadia felt a tremendous shuddering, starting from the epicentre of their coupling, but quickly spreading to every part of her, making her whole body shake with an exquisite and totally unfamiliar ecstasy. With an animal groan of pure release, she realised that Zayed had joined her and together they convulsed in a fever of gripping, sweaty, sated sexual fulfilment.

For several minutes they stayed like that, Zayed lying where he had fallen on top of her, his heart thumping heavily in a chest that was rising and falling from the exertion, sweat sealing their bodies together. Finally he rolled onto his side, taking her in his arms.

'Are you okay?' As he waited for his breath to slow down he swept away a strand of dark hair from Nadia's face. 'I wasn't too rough?'

'No, it was amazing!' The sight of her flushed cheeks and sparkling eyes gripped at something inside. 'You were amazing.'

'Why, thank you.' He leaned forward and gently ran a finger along her lips. 'And come to that, so were you.'

Suddenly he realised that she was. This woman, his wife, who he knew so little about, had just given him a sexual experience like no other he had ever known. And he had known more than his fair share. Her innocence, combined with the poised superiority and stunning body, was a killer combination he had never come across before.

'I know I have a lot to learn.'

'And believe me, it will give me the greatest of pleasure to teach you.' Laughing now, Zayed kissed away the serious words from her lips, pulling her into a closer embrace, and immediately felt the stirrings of sexual awakening starting again. It was this damned corset, he told himself as he found his hands running over the suspenders and round to her naked behind. How was any man meant to resist? His fingers touched something on her bare bottom and, peeling it off, he inspected the half-crushed rose petal before resting it on the tip of her upturned nose. Nadia twitched her nose in response, her eyes smiling, daring. 'Don't look at me like that, young lady,' he growled at her. 'Not if you want to get any sleep tonight.'

'I'm not sure that I do.' Squirming out of his grasp, Nadia reached forward to take hold of the cream satin coverlet, giving it a shake to dislodge more rose petals before lifting it so that it billowed up into the air and settled back down again over their hurriedly entwined bodies.

'I think sleeping is overrated.'

One thing you could never say about Nadia. In fact, he was starting to realise he might have seriously underrated this remarkable woman.

Nadia gazed at the beautiful man who slept so peacefully beside her now. The early-morning light was streaming in through the unshuttered windows, casting hexagonal patterns across a floor strewn with discarded undergarments and curling rose petals.

Carefully, so as not to waken him, she inched herself up against the pillows to be able to see him better. Last night had been incredible. The power of their lovemaking had moved her in a way that she hadn't thought possible. Now she watched as his eyes flickered beneath closed lids fringed by thick dark lashes. What was he dreaming? she wondered. This man whom she knew so little of, yet had tied herself to for life.

But if last night had proved one thing, it had been that Zayed was nothing like the cruel, heartless character her father had described. He was far from being the brutish animal she had been expecting; his lovemaking had been tender as well as passionate, fiery but so intimate, using his considerable skills to ensure that everything he did pleasured her as much as it did him. And it certainly had. She had had no idea that mere sex could take you to such wild levels of euphoria. She felt the stirrings of desire again now, just looking at him.

But overriding those feelings, overriding everything, in fact, was the torturous knowledge that today was the day she was going to have to confess who she was. Own up to the terrible truth that she wasn't from Gazbiyaa; she wasn't an ordinary girl on the run from an arranged marriage. She was Princess Nadia of Harith, only daughter of the sheikh of Harith, a man who viewed the kingdom of Gazbiyaa as his greatest enemy.

Everything she had done had been with the best of intentions. Fleeing the marriage of a man who would only have encouraged the war between Harith and Gazbiyaa. Marrying Sheikh Zayed Al Afzal in the desperate hope that she could stop it.

But right now she felt sick to the core about having to tell him the truth.

Slipping out of bed as quietly as possible, she went into the bathroom and returned wearing a bathrobe.

'Good morning.' Awake now, Zayed curved his lips into a sensual smile as he patted the bed beside him for her to rejoin him. 'How are you this morning?'

Nadia climbed up next to him and immediately Zayed pulled her towards him, kissing her firmly on the lips before snaking a hand under the dressing gown to her bare hip.

'Very well, thank you.' Nadia tried to smile back but her lips caught on her dry teeth, turning it into a half snarl. She moved up against the headboard, away from his touch. 'I suppose we should get up—there must be so much we have to do.'

A frown creased Zayed's brow as he propped himself on one elbow and, withdrawing his hand from under the dressing gown, ran it over his bearded jaw. 'I think we might be excused our duties on the first morning of our honeymoon.'

'Yes, of course.' She affected a laugh that sounded as false as it was.

'What's the matter?' He was staring at her intently now, frying her with his glare. 'What is it?'

*Oh, God.* This was it, then, she was going to have to tell him.

She looked down at him, at the short coarse hair that covered the sculpted planes of his olive-skinned torso, at the rippling muscled biceps of the arm he was leaning on. His body was so magnificent.

'Nadia?' He said her name sharply.

'There is…there is something I need to tell you.' This was so hard, so much harder than she could ever have imagined. The blood was roaring in her ears, muffling the sound of her words, threatening to blur her vision.

'Go ahead.' Harsh now, Zayed had pushed himself up so that he looked down on her, fixing her with eyes of such piercing intensity that they prickled her skin.

Nadia pulled the collar of her dressing gown tighter around her neck as she fought to find her voice.

'The thing is, I haven't been entirely truthful about who I really am.' The words were coming out in a rush of panic now. 'About where I come from.'

'Meaning what, exactly?'

'Meaning that I don't actually come from Gazbiyaa.'

'And where, *actually*, do you come from?'

Nadia gulped, her eyes cast down. There was nothing for it; she was just going to have to plunge right in.

'Harith.' The name stuck like a barb in her throat. 'I come from the kingdom of Harith.'

The silence that followed was so chilling, so deadly, that it felt to Nadia as if the world had frozen around her.

'Tell me that's not true.'

The force of his hissed words dragged her eyes upwards, but what she saw there made her shrink back with alarm. His face had turned thunderously dark, his eyes suddenly devoid of any light, any compassion, flint black.

She drew in a shuddering breath; her voice could only whisper its reply.

'It is true. I am Princess Nadia of Harith.'

# CHAPTER SIX

PRINCESS NADIA AMANI. Only daughter of the sheikh of Harith. His country's greatest enemy. The realisation of what he had done slammed into his chest. He had just made the biggest mistake of his life.

Ripping back the bedcover, Zayed grabbed his trousers from the floor and tugged them over his hips.

'Get up!'

'Look, Zayed, it's not what you think…'

'I said, get up!'

He turned away, not trusting himself to look at her, not trusting how the anger that was boiling inside him might make him behave.

But it was an anger directed largely at himself. He who prided himself on his good sense of judgement, his gut instinct. Well, he had gotten it wrong this time. Boy, had he got it wrong. And at a time when the stakes couldn't have been higher. Because this disastrous decision didn't just mean he was going to lose face and a few million dollars. His idiocy had put the lives of young men at risk, the young men of both Gazbiyaa and Harith.

'Zayed.' She was in front of him now. Standing there in that soft white robe, her black curls tumbling over her shoulders, her violet eyes flashing. 'If you would just let me explain—'

'Explain what? That you are a manipulative, calculating liar that has inveigled your way into my life in the most desperate way in order to wreak as much havoc as you can? I've worked that out for myself, thank you.'

'No, it's not like that, really—'

'That your plan has worked nicely, the gullible new sheikh immediately taken in by you, falling for your sob story about escaping an arranged marriage, looking for a different sort of life. Well, guess what? I know that, too.' He didn't know when he had ever felt so completely consumed with fury. It was roaring through his body, rooting him to the spot, his hands clenching and unclenching by his side. And having Nadia brazenly planted in front of him, refusing to back off and give his anger some space was only making matters worse. 'You may have tricked me into marriage, Nadia, but this is where the falsehoods end. I want you out of my life. Now.'

'No!' He watched her face go into shock, her hands fly to her burning cheeks. 'You don't mean that.'

'Either you leave of your own accord or I call security. Which is it to be?' He cast around for his discarded jacket and, retrieving his mobile phone from an inside pocket, held it aloft like a time bomb.

'But we are married. I am your wife.' Still she refused to move away from him, her bare feet planting her firmly on the floor, her arms now folded across her chest, her head held high. 'You can't just throw me out.'

'Just watch me.' He jerked back his head. 'The wedding will be annulled immediately.' But even as he said the words he knew that legally it would be near impossible. The union had been consummated. Nadia had made sure of that, hadn't she? The sickening realisation of just how much he had been manipulated, how much of a total sucker he had been, solidified the blood in his veins. She had totally played him.

'But last night... Didn't that mean anything to you?'

Well, she certainly wasn't going to be playing him any

more. No way was he going to be fooled by the hurt that she had managed to inject into those wide lilac eyes. Or the light tremble of the full bottom lip before it was nipped into stillness by a sharp tooth.

*She could win an award, this one.*

'Ha!' All his impotent rage and self-inflicted derision was poured into that one small word. He watched Nadia flinch. 'It was just sex, Nadia,' he forged on. 'Just one night of sex. Don't flatter yourself that it gives you any sort of hold over me. That you can add emotional blackmail to your list of deceptions.'

She turned away now, no doubt plotting her next move.

'Our marriage is over. You are leaving.' But suddenly he realised that just throwing her out was not enough. That alone on the streets of Gazbiyaa she would still be capable of creating all sorts of havoc. 'You will be returned to Harith.'

'Harith? No, not that!' She swung back now, the defiant composure gone, a deathly pallor creeping over her panic-stricken face.

'And just in case you should have any ideas of escaping, let me inform you that you will be accompanied by two of my most trusted guards who will know exactly the punishment awaiting them should my orders not be carried out successfully.'

*No!* Nadia felt the terror tightening her chest, clawing its way up to her throat. Was she to be evicted from the palace, transported back to Harith to meet her gruesome fate without being given any chance to explain? Was this really it?

She stared at the man in front of her. Her husband. He seethed with anger, shimmered with it. His trousers hung low around his hips, his taut abdominal muscles rippling beneath the broad expanse of his chest, the biceps of one arm flexing as he gripped the mobile phone in his hand.

Even though he was barefoot, he seemed to have grown in stature, as if his towering rage had added to his height.

Creeping through the fog of Nadia's panic came the black realisation that Zayed, this man she had married so optimistically, with such hope, was in fact no better than her father or her brother. He was treating her in just the way she had always been treated by the men in her life, like an object, to be used or discarded in any way they saw fit.

And it was this that gave her strength to stand up to him now. She clutched on to it like a raft of righteous indignation on the sea of terror to haul herself up. She refused to be cowed. And she certainly wasn't going to beg.

Steadfastly ignoring the look of hatred in Zayed's eyes, she concentrated on controlling every facial muscle to try to hide the misery of what he was doing to her. The very real terror of what was to become of her now.

'Fine. If this is how you want it, Zayed, I will go back to Harith. I will face my father and the consequences that that will bring. If your pride is more important than your kingdom, then I hope you are satisfied.'

'Don't you dare try to tell me how I feel about my kingdom.' Zayed was so angry he looked as if he might explode. 'I have sacrificed everything to be here, to become sheikh of Gazbiyaa. I am totally committed to my country.'

'Sacrifice?' Nadia immediately pounced on his admission. 'You don't know the meaning of the word!'

'I can assure you that I do.' His voice had dipped to a dangerous low. 'But it will be no *sacrifice* to remove you from my life. Let me tell you that.'

His vicious comment hurt—just as he had meant it to do—but Nadia refused to show him her pain. 'And does this *commitment* to your country include taking it to war? Having the blood of two nations on your hands? Because that is what will happen once my father hears that you and I are betrothed, that the marriage has been consummated, that I have been returned to Harith soiled by the hands of his greatest enemy.'

'Maybe you should have thought about that before you positioned yourself in my bed, before you started this whole, treacherous charade.' He shifted his position, crossing his arms over his bare chest. 'You have only brought this on yourself, Nadia.'

'Of course I thought about it.' Nadia matched his stance. 'But I didn't have any alternative. When I heard that you were to become sheikh instead of your warmonger of a brother I knew I had to seize the opportunity. That this would be, in all probability, the only chance I would ever have to make a difference, for my voice to be heard. I had to do what I did. No matter what the danger, what the *sacrifice*.'

'Very noble, I'm sure. And this voice that you are so keen to be heard, what exactly was it going to be saying? Reporting back to your father anything and everything that might be useful to help incite the war that Harith is so desperate to wage against Gazbiyaa?'

'No!'

'Gathering juicy bits of inside information, pillow talk that you could feed them to fuel their already insatiable desire for conflict?'

'No. You have no idea what you are talking about. I'm not a spy for my country. My father has no idea that I am here. If he did, believe me, our two countries would already be at war.'

'So what, then? Are you telling me that marrying me, the newly crowned sheikh of one of the wealthiest Arab states, was a prize worth the risk? That it was worth incurring the wrath of your own nation to become sheikha of Gazbiyaa for the life and privileges that would come with that title?'

A heated loathing flooded Nadia's body, strangling her

vocal cords, misting her eyes. How could she ever have thought she might have had any feelings for this man?

'Do you honestly think you are so big a prize that I would risk not only my own life but the lives of my countrymen just to be with you?' She gave him a look of complete and utter contempt, her fists balled by her sides, her nails digging into her palms. 'Perhaps one day you should try to peer over the top of your mountain-size ego and see the world beyond it. You have no idea, do you, about the ways of our countries, how to rule a kingdom like Gazbiyaa, how to prevent a catastrophic war?'

'And you do, I suppose?'

'Yes. Yes, I do. At least, I am prepared to do anything and everything I can to try to find peace. That's what I am doing here, Zayed. That's why I broke into your bedroom, why I wanted to be made sheikha of Gazbiyaa. Because by being at the heart of this kingdom I thought I could influence the decisions being made about the future of mine.'

Nadia paused, her breath coming in short bursts, rasping in her throat, roughening her voice. 'So you see I have no interest in you or your wealth or your extravagant lifestyle. In fact I have nothing but contempt for it. Because I can see the man it has made you—vain and egotistical, a man whose pride is more important to him than his people.'

'That's enough!' Zayed raised his hand to silence her, his voice thundering around the room. 'I will not allow you to speak to me like that.'

'I shall speak to you how I like.' Nadia hadn't finished with him yet. 'You can inflict no greater punishment on me than returning me to Harith. My *crime* will be punishable by death. You will have my blood on your hands, Zayed, but far worse than that, you will also have the blood of our two nations.'

There was sharp silence. Zayed stared at Nadia, at this fireball of passion and fury and misguided morality, if indeed that was what it was. Her spirited defence had annoyed the hell out of him but it had felt genuine, as if it had come from the heart. That she really had done all this because of some crazy idea that she could prevent a war between their two countries.

And the fear on her face when he had told her she would be returning to Harith…there had been no mistaking that. The way the colour had drained alarmingly from her skin, the wide-eyed terror in her eyes, the slight sway when her knees had threatened to give way beneath her, making him want to stretch out to catch her before she had quickly steadied herself. Could she have put that on? And then faked the way she had tried to cover it up with all that defiant rhetoric? His instincts told him no, it had been genuine. But then, it was his instincts that had got him into this accursed mess. Had got him married to probably the most dangerously unsuitable woman on the planet.

He needed some time to think. To get his head round what he had done and come up with a solution, as fast as possible. But first he needed to get Nadia out of his sight.

Because despite everything, despite the bitterness and betrayal and downright fury with himself that he could ever have been such a fool, seeing her standing before him now still turned him on. At some time during her passionate tirade the belt of her gown had loosened, revealing a flash of naked thigh and the swell of rounded breasts—breasts that he knew fitted perfectly into his cupped palm, tasted so sweet against his lips, whose nipples puckered so readily with arousal. He would only have to take a step forward, slip the gown down over her shoulders and lower his head…

And then he would be in even more trouble. Hell! Just when had he become so weak? Cursing under his breath, he raised his phone and with one jab was through to security.

'Yes....The bridal bedroom....Rani and Ahmed....Right away.'

He turned to look at a now silent Nadia, and there it was again, that fleeting flash of fear in her eyes before the shoulders went back and the fear was immediately masked with rebellious defiance. And she held his gaze, so determined, so strong-willed, refusing to even let herself blink. It was a long hard stare that scorched the air between them.

'Your Royal Highness?' The guards had arrived, entering the room on Zayed's command, muscles flexed, ready for action. They halted, looking around them, bewildered for a moment as they took in the scene: the passion-rumpled bed, the new sheikha, flushed and dishevelled, now clutching her robe to her body. And the sheikh, bare-chested and rigid with tension, barely controlling his anger.

'You will escort the sheikha to her quarters.'

'Sire.'

'And once there you will stand guard over her until you receive further instructions. Do you understand?'

'Yes, sire.'

Despite their unquestioning acceptance, there was an awkward moment when the guards looked at Nadia, unsure how to proceed. Nadia glared back at them defiantly.

'Take. Her. Away.' Zayed snarled the words and they immediately lurched into action, moving in muscled unison to lift Nadia off her feet and turn her towards the door.

'Don't worry, I'm going anyway.' Defiant to the last, Nadia spat the words over her shoulder, her bare feet furiously paddling the air beneath her as she was borne away. 'Believe me, nothing would persuade me to stay here now.' As the guards negotiated the doorway she took the opportunity to shoot Zayed one final, venomous glare. 'Because now I know the man you really are, Sheikh Zayed Al Afzal. For all your posturing, your clever words, you are no better than my father and brother. You are nothing more than a wolf in designer clothing.'

And with that final insult she was gone.


Nadia paced around the suite of rooms that had been hers since she'd arrived at the palace of Gazbiyaa. Since she had somehow, miraculously, found herself engaged to the sheikh and been so hopeful that her plan might actually work, that she really might be able to make a difference.

Now that plan lay in tatters, along with the rest of her life—what was left of it. She hadn't been exaggerating when she had told Zayed what punishment would await her in Harith.

For she had brought the utmost shame on the kingdom of Harith—if running away from an arranged marriage wasn't bad enough, she had then married the ruler of their greatest enemy, been deflowered and then rejected by him. It didn't get any worse than that. If she had deliberately set out to disgrace their family she couldn't have done a better job. And even though she knew her poor mother would plead with her husband and son to spare her daughter's life, her words would fall on deaf ears. Because Harithian women were not afforded the privilege of an opinion. Any more than the sheep and camels that made up their dowries.

Sinking down onto the edge of the bed, she put her head in her hands, threading her fingers through the hair falling over her forehead, pressing the heels of her palms into her eye sockets. On the other side of the heavy panelled door stood the two guards, waiting to be told what to do with her. There was nothing she could do now except await her fate.

Her feverish mind had run through every possibility she could think of to make an escape: from bribing the guards with promises of riches she didn't have or sexual favours she would never give them to leaping out of the sky-high window and hoping for the best. Maybe ending up splattered on the scorching white pavement below would be the kindest thing.

Hearing the guards moving outside the door and the key turn in the lock, Nadia took in a shuddering breath to rein in the terror. This was it, then. If nothing else, she was determined that she would go with her head held high.

She looked ridiculously small, flanked on either side by the guards that had her brought her to him. But what Nadia lacked in stature she certainly made up for in courage, her posture upright, her chin held high, those intense eyes trained on him with undisguised hatred.

Dismissing the guards, Zayed gestured to Nadia to sit beside him on one of the *kelim* cushions arranged around a low coffee table on this shady terrace. He had needed to be outside, to be able to breathe some air into lungs choked with the enormity of what he had done.

And the calm vista before him had helped. He had chosen a spot well away from the scene of last night's celebrations, where the tented structures were being dismantled right now, fervently wishing that his marriage could be dismantled so easily.

He had stared at his kingdom, through the rainbow sprinklers of the manicured lawns, past the fountains and statues and the swaying palm trees to the broad sweep of the Sarawat Mountains on the horizon, a soft, jagged purple against the scorching sky. And between him and them had been the vast expanse of desert.

He had made his decision. He didn't trust Nadia; he would never be able to trust her. He now knew he was married to a woman who was capable of such deception that she would stop at nothing to achieve her aim, whatever that aim was.

He had been over and over their earlier confrontation, tying his brain in knots trying to figure it out. His first thought, that she had invaded his life solely to stir up trouble, that she was hell-bent on bringing their two kingdoms to war, just didn't add up, no matter which way he looked at it.

It was possible that she being used as a pawn. Forced by her family to infiltrate the palace of Gazbiyaa, with the threat of whatever barbaric punishments a country like Harith saw fit to administer if she didn't do as she was told. But then, why would she have confessed to him who she was? And besides, even though it had turned out that he knew virtually nothing about the woman he had married, the one thing that could never be in question was her sheer courage. It surrounded her like a force field. Zayed refused to believe that Nadia would ever be anybody's puppet.

That had only left one option. That she had been telling the truth. That she really had risked everything to come here without her family's knowledge to try to prevent the war between their two kingdoms. That would certainly explain the look of terror on her face at the thought of being returned. But even if that was the case, it was every bit as dangerous as the other scenarios. Because her deluded, misguided action had dramatically increased the likelihood of war.

And there was something else. Something he could hardly bring himself to admit. Try as he might to deny it, this woman had inexplicably gotten to him, sneaked under his armour plating of emotional indifference to somewhere deep inside him that had never been touched before. Somewhere raw and new. Somewhere he didn't even want to think about. And that made her as dangerous to him as a tank full of hungry sharks.

He had to sort this out. Now.

* * *

Nadia folded herself elegantly onto a cushion as far away from Zayed as she could get. She didn't know what she was doing here. If he was expecting some grovelling apology, then he was going to be sorely disappointed. If he wanted her to plead to be allowed to stay, well, he was out of luck there too. Because she wanted nothing more to do with this man. The tentative faith she had put in him had been cruelly slashed. Now that he had shown her his true colours she just wanted to get away from him, from Gazbiyaa. She would rather meet her fate than spend any more time in his company. Well, that was what her pride was telling her, at least.

She raised her eyes to look at him, determined not to show any weakness now. But it was a weakness of a different kind that lanced through her poor, mentally tortured body. Because seeing Zayed now, calmly pouring coffee from the brass pot on the table, made something shift inside her, something indefinable, primal. It had only been a few hours since they had spent the night together, since they had shared such incredible intimacy. Zayed's hard, muscled, sweat-slicked body wrapped around her, hungry for her, seeming to not be able to get enough of her. Nadia could still feel the thrilling weight of him on top of her, hear the rasp of his heated breath, the groan of his release. And the burn of her own body where he had been was an actual, physical reminder of what they had done.

But now it was as if they were strangers. Cold and remote, he handed her a cup of coffee, his posture stiff, the sharp planes of his cheekbones hollowing to the angular line of his jaw, held firm beneath its close-cropped, dark beard. The anger had gone, replaced with an unspoken, chilling authority.

'So…' Nadia said, replacing her rattling coffee cup back on the table. 'What do you want to see me about? Because if this is some sort of farewell gesture, then you needn't bother. You might think you can assuage your conscience, justify your actions with a few mealy-mouthed words to make yourself feel better, but let me tell you it won't make any difference—'

'Nadia!'

'—because ultimately you will be answerable to your own conscience.' Her diatribe suddenly lost its momentum beneath the searing intensity of Zayed's glare.

'Have you quite finished?'

Nadia opened her mouth but quickly closed it again, Zayed's raised-palm gesture making it quite clear he didn't want to hear the answer.

'I have brought you here to tell you that I am going to allow you to stay.'

'Stay?'

'Yes, stay here in Gazbiyaa. For the time being at least. You will not be returning to Harith.'

'Oh.' Nadia felt a tidal wave of relief wash over her. But her pride refused to let it show. 'And supposing I don't want to stay?'

It was only the smallest of movements, but the way Zayed leaned forward and narrowed his eyes sent a chill of alarm through her. She had poked an already angry tiger, and he looked as if he was about to pounce.

'Let's get this clear, shall we? I have *zero* interest in what you want. It would give me the greatest pleasure to remove you from Gazbiyaa, to get you out of my life once and for all. But your actions have placed our two countries in the most tremendous peril. If the news gets out that the sheikh of Gazbiyaa has married a Harithian princess, it will mean certain war. My urgent priority now is to find a way to minimise the damage.'

'But it was never my intention to…'

The blaze in his eyes stopped her in her tracks.

'I need to buy some time to try to establish diplomatic relations with Harith. So this is what is going to happen now. Listen carefully.'

Nadia nodded mutely.

'First, no one must ever know that you are from Harith. *Ever.* Do I make myself clear?'

She nodded again.

'We have to keep your identity hidden for as long as we can. I have ordered that the official wedding photographs be "mistakenly" destroyed, and personal photography was banned, so with luck we can keep any images out of the press. No one seems to know who you are as yet, but this is a secret that we must guard with our lives.'

'Of course, I understand.' Beneath the smouldering hostility she could see the worry etched across his handsome features as he tried to tackle the enormity of the problem. A problem that at the moment she had simply exacerbated. If only he would let her in, let her help, she was so sure she could. 'I won't breathe a word to anyone about who I really am.'

'You had better not. For your own sake, as well as for the sake of your country.'

'I know that.' Pushing back her shoulders, Nadia fought her corner. 'You hardly need to spell that out to me.'

'Well, maybe there are some things that I do need to spell out.' He gave her a punishing stare. 'From now on, Nadia, you and I are going to be playing the part of the perfect couple. To the outside world, the sheikh and his new bride are madly in love, totally devoted to one another, publicly displaying the sort of happiness that will soon produce a royal heir and the stability that this country so desperately needs.'

'Yes, of course.' Something about the tone of his voice suggested that there was more to come.

'Privately, however—' his voice lowered with chilling authority '—privately things will be very different. This will be a marriage in name only. A marriage that will be terminated as soon as it is safe to do so. Behind closed doors there will be no relationship between us. Do I make myself clear?'

Nadia tossed back her head, the blue-black waves of her lustrous hair rippling down her back as she took a moment to arrange her features, to banish any sign of emotion.

'Yes, Zayed.' Her voice was cold and steady. 'Perfectly clear.'

# CHAPTER SEVEN

'Here you are.'

Nadia looked up as Zayed strode into the library, his presence immediately dominating the room. He was wearing jeans that sat low on his hips and a plain white T-shirt that stretched across the broad expanse of his chest, flexed biceps bulging beneath the tight sleeves. Nadia looked back down again.

'You haven't forgotten we are dining with the foreign affairs minister and his wife this evening?'

'No, I haven't forgotten.' Nadia closed the beautiful illuminated manuscript on her lap. She could spend hours here in the library, carefully leafing through their priceless pages, the brightly coloured paintings and meticulously handwritten text. Which was just as well, because there was precious little else for her to do in this gilded cage she found herself in.

'It's informal, but obviously you are going to need time to change.' His gaze raked over her figure, dressed in a simple pale blue shift dress, her long legs tucked under her as she had made herself comfortable in the high-backed leather armchair.

'Obviously.' Placing the book reverentially on the table beside her, Nadia unfurled her legs and sat up straight, raising her watchful eyes to his once more. 'And presumably you are, too.'

Zayed took a step towards her, then stopped. 'Look, Nadia. There is no point in being like this.'

'Like what?' Busying herself with untucking her hair from behind her ears and casually flicking it so that it tumbled over her shoulders, Nadia pointedly didn't return his gaze. 'I wasn't aware that I was being like anything.'

'You know exactly what I mean.' Zayed was right in front of her now, looking down on her. His height towered over her, solid, powerful, sexy, and Nadia felt her limbs weaken, the way they always did when she was close to him, a feeling she had been battling to control ever since this so called arrangement of theirs had begun.

It had been three weeks now, three long, torturous weeks, each one worse than the one before. Far from settling into her fake role as the adoring young bride, Nadia was finding it more and more frustrating, more and more impossible to cope with. Her relationship with Zayed was already strained to breaking point. How on earth was she supposed to carry on with this ridiculous charade until he decided he had solved the problem of Harith? And what would happen to her after that? The powerlessness of her situation kept her awake at night, churning round and around her sleepless brain.

And her sense of isolation was growing every day, too. Totally cut off from her own country and virtually ignored by her husband, she was starting to wonder if she had fallen into some sort of parallel universe where she didn't really exist at all. That the real Nadia was somewhere else, living her boringly restrictive life, while this one, the one who spent her lonely days wandering the echoing corridors of this vast palace or shut away here in the library, was just a cardboard cut-out of the real thing.

She might just as well be for all the good she was doing. Any hopes that she would be able to influence Zayed's decisions, play a part in the peace process, had been dashed at the onset. The sheikh had made it quite clear that her opinions were of no interest to him, that her role was solely to keep quiet and look decorative whenever the occasion demanded it. The role, in fact, that she had always had mapped out for her by her father. An irony that wasn't lost on her.

But along with this huge frustration was the other thing, the *thing* that Nadia had tried so hard to ignore but which kept coming back to slap her in the face. Zayed. Just that. *Him.* The night they had spent together, the things they had done, haunting her with their vivid images, greedily pervading her consciousness at any time of the day or night, no matter how often she expressly forbade herself from going there.

Being in the same room as him was agony. Just the sound of his voice was enough to set her heart rate pounding, her skin tingling with a thousand skittery pinpricks if he so much as stood beside her or brushed past her. And when he pulled her to him, slipping an arm around her waist in a show of affection for the benefit of whoever it was he was trying to convince at the time, her traitorous body leaped into full take-me-I'm-yours mode, jelly legs, clenching stomach muscles, the lot. Even though she *knew* that his gesture was totally fake. Knew that in reality, rather than pulling her closer to him, he would have liked to push her far enough away so that he never had to see her again. To the edge of a cliff, maybe. One with a crumbling edge...

And it was happening again right now, that hollow yearning feeling creeping over her as she stared at the chest of this man, at the breadth of his shoulders, the defined muscles of his neck. Nadia hated herself for it, for her pathetic weakness where he was concerned, a man who had nothing but bitter contempt for her. And that made her as spiky as a cactus, which was presumably what Zayed was referring to now.

'D'you know what, Nadia?' He jammed a hand into his jeans' pocket, his thumb pushed through the belt loop as his dismissive gaze raked over her. 'Your manner baffles me. Bearing in mind that you got us into this mess, I fail to see why I'm being treated like the bad guy. Quite frankly, in your position I thought you would be doing everything you could to try to make this arrangement work.'

'I do as I'm told.' Nadia pouted back at him. 'That's what you want, isn't it?'

'I want you to lose the attitude.'

'Then, maybe you should try changing yours.' Immediately on the defensive, Nadia rose to her feet to challenge him, only to realise that they were too close together now, far too close. She edged back as far as the chair would let her. 'If you would listen to what I have to say rather than treating me like some sort of pariah, if you would let me—'

'Stop right there, Nadia.' Zayed's forceful words were accompanied by a dark scowl and raised palm as he moved in closer. 'The sooner you wise up to the fact that you are here on my terms, the better it will be for all concerned. While you are living under my roof here in Gazbiyaa, you will do as I say. You have no rights, no bargaining power, your opinions count for nothing. So you can keep them to yourself until you are back in your precious Harith, back where you belong.'

His vituperative words simmered between them, momentarily silencing Nadia with their deliberately wounding attack. She swallowed, looking away from him, lowering her lashes as she waited for the stinging pain of the rebuke to recede.

Meanwhile she heard Zayed clear his throat. 'I take it you haven't heard anything from your family?'

'No,' Nadia answered petulantly, taking another step back until the chair was pressing into her bare calves. 'How would I? They have no way of contacting me.'

'But they must be searching for you?'

'I assume so.'

'Do you think they might have any idea where you are?'

'Well, I haven't exactly been sending them postcards.' Her acerbic reply was purely a defence mechanism, an attempt to deflect the dreadful thought that her family were probably scouring the length and breadth of Harith and beyond in order to try to track her down. Or, more surprising, the hollow emptiness that they might not. But as she raised her eyes to the sight of Zayed's jaw visibly clenching she quickly backtracked. 'No, I don't think they have any idea. If my family had discovered where I was we would know about it by now. Gazbiyaa is the last place they would be looking for me.'

'Well, that's something, I suppose,' Zayed said. 'But it's only a matter of time before they figure it out. You need to make sure that word doesn't get out before I find a solution to this fiasco.'

'I know that. You don't need to keep reminding me.'

'Perhaps I wouldn't have to if you started to show a bit more gratitude.'

'What?'

'You heard.'

'Gratitude?' Nadia repeated the word with disgust. 'Is *that* what you want from me, Zayed?'

'Maybe. Yes, why not? I don't think that's unreasonable. Given the circumstances.' He shot her a laser stare. 'You ought to be very thankful to be allowed to stay here in the palace where you have the security of twenty-four-hour protection, not to mention every comfort. Especially when you consider what the alternative might have been. I would say I have treated you with remarkable tolerance.'

'Well, thank you so much for that.' Sarcasm leeched from Nadia's words. 'Forgive me for not realising that simpering gratitude was in order. Presumably your other women were only too happy to grovel on their knees for your favours.'

She faltered. Where had that come from? The last thing she wanted was for him to think she cared about his past relationships. That she cared about him at all, in fact.

'My "other women", as you put it, have never tricked and lied their way into my life, into a marriage with potentially disastrous consequences for all concerned.' Zayed had immediately pounced on her indiscretion, as she'd known he would. 'I think that puts you into a different league altogether, wouldn't you say?'

Nadia scowled back at him. She was sick and tired of being reminded of what she had done, of being told that she was the villain of the piece but refused any opportunity to justify her actions.

And what was more, she hated the way he had said 'other women', even though she had started it. Said from his lips, it made his past seem more real, and it was a past she was trying to blot out. Which was difficult when her image of a woman on her hands and knees in front of him refused to go away. An image that now saw them both naked.

She needed to focus. Get back on track. 'Maybe if you spent more time thinking about how I could help with the situation and less time blaming me for it, we could make some progress.' This was more like it. 'All the gratitude in the world won't make any difference to that.'

'Fine.' Zayed squared his shoulders. 'As you are so keen to help, you can start by playing the role of the perfect hostess this evening, by being the devoted wife. No matter how much that pains you.' He glared at her pointedly. 'Hassan Rouhani is an important political figure on the world stage and I need to make sure that he is on side. Handled correctly he will be a useful ally, but only if I can impress upon him that Gazbiyaa is safe in my hands. That I have the situation with Harith under control.'

Nadia made a small noise in her throat, but the warning flash in Zayed's eyes halted its escape.

'Your job is to entertain…Fatima.'

'Salema. His wife is called Salema.'

'Whatever. You need to make sure she thinks our marriage is rock solid, that the future of the royal line is assured.'

'Certainly, sire. Perhaps you would like me to stuff a cushion up my dress.'

'That won't be necessary.'

Zayed turned away, biting down hard on his bottom lip to stop the smile from forming. How could he even think about finding this situation amusing? Nadia was the most exhausting, infuriating, exasperating woman who he had ever had the misfortune to meet. And yet he seemed to keep coming back for more. Here he was, trying to convince high-ranking dignitaries that he had everything under control, when, truth be told, he couldn't even control his wife.

'Well, I must say it does my heart good to see a young couple so much in love.' Perhaps stupefied by the several courses of rich food, Salema Rouhani leaned back in her chair and surveyed her companions around the table. 'Don't you think so, Hassan? Don't they make a lovely couple?'

'Quite charming, my dear.' Hassan Rouhani was small in stature, but his lack of height was compensated by sharp, inquisitive eyes and a keen mind. Nadia had immediately sensed that their acting skills were going to have to ramp up a notch for this man, that he wouldn't be as easy to fool as the many other dignitaries she had had to entertain in her short time here. Beyond casting an eye over her very obvious attributes, they had appeared to take little interest in her. 'And no doubt the people of Gazbiyaa are happy

to see their sheikh married. It shows commitment, investment in the future.' His eyes twinkled knowingly, as if he
understood exactly why Zayed had taken a bride so suddenly. 'Especially now, during a period of such instability.'

Nadia looked away from his direct gaze and picked up
her glass of water. Hassan might have thought he'd sussed
them out, but he only knew part of the story.

'That reminds me,' Hassan continued. 'I have heard a
rumour that Azeed is in Harith. Has he been in contact
with you, Zayed?'

At the name *Harith* Nadia started, the gulp of water
she had just taken going down the wrong way, leaving her
spluttering and choking.

Salema was up on her feet in a second, thwacking Nadia
completely unnecessarily between the shoulder blades
while Nadia raised her hands in what she hoped was a
semaphore version of 'I'm perfectly all right, thank you.'
When she had finally recovered enough to breathe again,
she raised her mascara-smudged eyes, only to be faced
with the twin stares of the men at the table. Hassan's bird-
like focus conveyed a distinct interest in the little scene
that had just been played out before him, while Zayed had
narrowed his to darkly lashed weapons of mass destruction, leaving Nadia in no doubt that she was spluttering
her way into very dangerous territory.

'No, I've heard nothing from Azeed.' With calm re-
stored, Zayed returned to Hassan's question. 'He has completely ignored my attempts to make peace, to get some
dialogue going between us. I've decided if that is his final
decision I will have to respect it.'

'Well, if he is in Harith it could make things very difficult for you. The more ammunition Harith have to use
against Gazbiyaa, the more dangerous the situation becomes. My advice would be to find a diplomatic solution
as quickly as possible.'

'Come, dear.' Salema stretched out an arm to Nadia. 'This is our cue to leave the men to their business. Shall we take our tea in the salon?'

'Actually, I would like to hear this conversation.' Nadia gave a small cough, blatantly ignoring the don't-you-dare-go-there vibes that were zinging her way from Zayed. 'How can you reach a diplomatic solution when the two countries refuse to communicate with one another?'

'Indeed.' Leaning forward, Hassan linked his fingers and rested his chin on them, regarding her speculatively. 'And how would you suggest that problem could be solved?'

'I'm sure she has no idea, do you, Nadia?' Zayed bit out her name through gritted teeth.

'I do have an idea, actually. I think the solution would be for both sides to sit round a table together and decide to end this conflict. The problems and grievances need to be thrashed out verbally, and I don't mean with chest beating and threats of war, I mean talked through logically and sensibly. There would need to be a mediator there to ensure fairness, but, more important, the very best advisors should be utilised to help find ways to achieve lasting peace. And by that I don't mean government bureaucrats sitting in their lofty towers... No offence...'

'None taken.' Hassan bit back a smile. 'Go on—what sort of advisors do you have in mind?'

'People who know the situation, preferably from both sides, people who really understand the hearts and minds of the two kingdoms and who are committed to peace. Who can persuade both nations to put aside their pride and channel that energy into building a positive relationship between Gazbiyaa and Harith, both now and in the future.'

Speech done, Nadia sat back in her chair, her cheeks flushed, her heart hammering in her chest. The table around her seemed to have gone very quiet, the only noise being her own blood roaring in her ears.

Finally the silence was broken by a slow handclap by Hassan, followed by a hearty guffaw. 'Well said, young lady.' He turned to Zayed, who appeared to have been struck frighteningly dumb. 'This is some wife you have found yourself here, Zayed—beauty and brains and a fighting spirit, as well. You are a lucky man.'

'Aren't I just?' The gritted teeth had turned to full-on lockjaw, the sheer force of his hostility dragging Nadia's gaze from where it had settled in her lap up to his murderous, blazing brown eyes. Nadia blinked against their force, and looked away again, suddenly finding the gold bracelet around her wrist unusually fascinating. 'She's certainly full of surprises.'

'Forgive me, Salema.' Nadia hastily turned to her companion. 'I am keeping us from our tea.' Suddenly she couldn't get away from the table, away from Zayed, fast enough. She rose to standing and the others followed suit. Taking Salema's arm, she started to guide her from the room.

'Have I said what a lovely colour your dress is?' She could feel Zayed's eyes burning a hole into the back of her head. 'Such a pretty blue.'


'What the hell was all that about?'

With a sharp rap on the door, Zayed had come storming into Nadia's bedroom, which was positioned at the far end of their private suite, about as far away from his own room as possible. He had brought his cloud of fury with him.

'Did I not make it clear to you, only today, that under no circumstances were you to speak about Harith?' His rant had carried him to the middle of the room where he stopped with his hands on his hips, his breathing heavy. Nadia was seated at the dressing table, wearing a satin camisole-and-shorts set, her hairbrush held in the air, mid-stroke. The sight of her did nothing to ease his breathing.

'You do know that thanks to your little outburst Rouhani is going to work out who you are, where you are from? It was bad enough drawing attention to yourself with that choking episode, but then to subject us all to your half-baked opinions of how to solve the problem of Harith…' His jaw worked forcibly. 'Why didn't you just hold up a sign, Nadia? One with a big arrow saying, "Look at me, I'm from Harith".'

'If I may finally be allowed to say something.' The hair-brush was being pointed at him like a weapon as she swung herself round on the wooden stool, lifting her buttocks to free the skimpy bit of satin fabric that hadn't turned with her. Zayed swallowed hard.

'First, it was hardly my fault that I choked on a sip of water. It wasn't as though I did it on purpose. And second, why shouldn't I speak out, put forward some ideas? Somebody needs to do something.'

'*I* am dealing with it, Nadia,' Zayed growled, struggling to rein in his temper. 'You "speaking out", as you put it, is only increasing the pressure, increasing the danger, making my job all the more hellishly difficult. Why can't you see that?'

'So you are dealing with it, are you? And exactly what progress are you making?'

'I am *not* accountable to you, young lady.' The blood in his veins was heating up, nearing boiling point. How dare she start cross-examining him when she had been the one who had escalated the crisis—who seemed to be intent on putting them in even more danger? How dare she even look like that, her scantily clad body twisted round to glare at him, all soft skin and lithe limbs, the satin shorts pulled tight over her crossed thighs, disappearing between her legs? 'Your part of the deal, since you seem to have forgotten, is to be the adoring sheikha, keep a low profile, and, most important, keep *quiet*.' The last word was snapped at her through clenched teeth.

'But the quieter I keep, the more loudly I can hear the sabre rattling on both sides.' The hairbrush was now being waved at him for emphasis. 'Something has to be done, Zayed, right away, before the blood of our young men is spilled.'

'Don't you think I know that?' His temper had taken him several steps towards her so that he was now before her, looking down with fire burning in his eyes. 'Don't you think I am doing everything in my power to prevent that, to make sure it doesn't happen?'

'No, I don't.'

*'What?'*

Nadia banged the hairbrush back down on the dressing table. Then, raising herself to standing, she pushed back her shoulders.

'I said I don't think that you are doing everything you can to bring about peace.' Her voice was calm and controlled but there was a tremor there, too. There was no doubt how much this meant to her. 'You are so busy setting up meetings with the great and the good that you can't see what is right in front of you.' She stamped a small bare foot down to the floor to make her point.

Zayed could see exactly what was right in front of him. He was struggling to control the waves of undiluted lust it was causing.

Before him stood the most beautiful young woman he had ever known, lustrous black hair falling in waves around her shoulders, bright eyes flashing and cheeks flushed with passionate self-righteousness. One thin strap of the flimsy top she was wearing had slipped down, and try as he might Zayed couldn't stop his eyes from travelling to the swell of her breasts, from lingering at the sight of the erect nipples beneath the satin fabric. Try as he might he couldn't stop the throb of arousal in his groin.

'Because I am the best advisor you are ever going to

find!' If Nadia had noticed the effect she was having on him she didn't show it, too caught up in the conviction of her beliefs. 'I know more about Harith than any of these so-called experts that you are wasting your time talking to. If only you would stop behaving like a chauvinistic, sexist pig, stop blaming me for everything and start listening to what I have to say, together we might find a solution.'

'Okay, that's enough! This conversation is over.' Zayed took a step away, needing to find the space and control to fight the twin battles Nadia was waging: one severely testing his patience, the other his rampant masculinity.

It was the latter that was screaming at him to sweep this arrogant, insubordinate young woman off her stamping feet, cross the few steps to her bed, lay her down and make love to her. And once that idea had formed in his head it had very quickly spread to his lower regions where it firmly, very firmly refused to go away.

Mentally he was on top of her, looking down at her luscious body, sliding his hand down to those flimsy satin shorts and pulling them down over her hips. Or maybe leaving them on, pushing the leg of the shorts to one side so that he had access to that most intimate part of her body with his fingers, then swapping his fingers for the throbbing member that was straining against his suit trousers right now, positioning himself so that he could lower down onto her, thrust into her, feel the mixture of her dampness, the soft skin and the coarser hair and the satin fabric rubbing between them.

Hell! Furious with himself, Zayed turned and took several long strides towards the door. What ever was the matter with him? This woman was totally off-limits and yet he was behaving like a hormone-raging teenager.

'Don't you dare walk away from me.'

Nadia's imperious voice halted his step, and he half turned to look at her over his shoulder.

'Quite the little princess, aren't we?' His voice was sharp, eyes glittering coldly. 'Stamping your feet and telling me what to do. You are not in Harith now, Nadia. I'm not one of your minions that you can order around. When you made the decision to come here to "claim" me for your husband, you forwent that privilege. Perhaps I should remind you that you are my wife now, on paper at least, and as such you will do as I say, not the other way round. From the moment you signed that marriage certificate you became my—'

'What?' Nadia had darted round in front of him, blocking his exit, all flushed cheeks, tousled hair and flashing eyes. 'Go on, say it. I became your property. That's what you were about to say, wasn't it? That I belong to you. I am just another one of your possessions in the same way women have been treated for generations by both your family and mine. How could I have deluded myself that you were any different?'

'I was actually going to say you became my responsibility.' Nadia blinked back at him, momentarily wrong-footed. 'But if we are dealing with home truths maybe I should come up with a better word. You became a liability, Nadia, that's what. A dangerous liability.'

He watched as she bit down on the pout of her lower lip, her pearly white teeth nipping into its luscious pink softness as she fought to control the tremble his words had produced. Suddenly the sight of her, in all her vulnerable, fiery sexiness, unwittingly tormenting him in that scrap of an outfit, was too much for him. He had to get away. *Now.* Before he did something he would seriously regret.

Purposefully moving past her, he reached the safety of the doorway, willing himself to keep walking. Never before had he felt temptation like this.

# CHAPTER EIGHT

'I HAD AN email from Hassan Rouhani this morning.'

Zayed had waited for the two staff who were serving their food to leave before he spoke. He and Nadia were sitting at the small round table in the informal dining room, something they did most evenings in an effort to keep up the pretence of the happily married couple. Tonight that effort was doubly difficult with last night's heated confrontation still smarting between them.

Nadia had not seen Zayed all day, as per usual, and with nothing to do except reflect on her 'little outburst' of the night before, as Zayed had so furiously labelled it, she had started to wonder if maybe he was right, maybe she had made things worse by speaking out. It looked as if she was about to find out.

'What did he say?' She laid down her knife and fork, her appetite for the *sayadieh samak*, the delicious-smelling baked fish and rice on her plate, suddenly vanishing.

'Oh, glowing praise.' He levelled those deep brown eyes at her. 'For you, that is. Positively gushing with congratulations that I have managed to find myself such a charming and intelligent wife.'

'That's good.' Nadia would have loved to savour this morsel of victory, but Zayed's tone, his unspoken *if only he knew*, was robbing her of any triumph. She tried shooting him a meaningful glance instead. 'It's nice that someone appreciates me.'

'Isn't it just?'

Nadia lowered her eyes to the safety of her plate. 'Did he say anything else?' She casually picked up her fork again.

'If you mean did he say he knows who you are, then no. But don't think that lets you off the hook. Rouhani is a clever man—he may well have decided there is no benefit in showing his hand, or maybe he's going to do some more investigation. Either way, what you said last night was totally irresponsible.'

Nadia sighed. Did this man never take a break from telling her off? 'Well, I liked him.'

'How nice. Perhaps you should start a mutual admiration society.'

She let her gaze flick back to him, surprised by what sounded almost like jealousy. No, she instantly dismissed that thought. That would be ridiculous.

'Did Hassan say any more about Azeed? Do you really think he is in Harith?'

'Who knows?' Zayed concentrated on his meal.

'So he has refused to have any contact with you?'

'That is correct.' Now he scowled. Perhaps Nadia would like him to pass the salt so she could rub it directly into the wound. 'Are you intending to eat anything this evening or just ask a lot of annoying questions?'

'That must be hard for you.' Nadia deliberately ignored him. 'To have your brother cut you out of his life through no fault of your own.' He replied with a wall of silence but still she persevered. 'Were you close—growing up, I mean?'

'Not especially.' Finally Zayed raised his eyes to look at her. It seemed she wasn't going to give up, determined to turn over the stones to expose his weaknesses and failures. He hardened his voice. 'Our upbringing was very different. Azeed was educated here in Gazbiyaa, groomed all his life for the role of sheikh, whereas I was sent to board-

ing school in England. As the second son I had much more
freedom. I was able to pursue my own career, control my
own destiny. Until now, that is.'

He stopped abruptly. He could see Nadia assimilating
the information, her beautiful head tilted to one side, her
amethyst-coloured eyes perceptive and alert. He already
regretted the emphasis he had put on his last few words. He
knew she was never going to let that go. And he was right.

'But now you are the sheikh of Gazbiyaa.' Her eyes took
on the challenge. 'Surely there can be no greater honour
than to be ruler of your kingdom?'

'But that honour comes at a price.'

'You mean your relationship with your brother?'

'Well, partly that.' Guiltily Zayed realised he was only
just beginning to recognise how much that rift hurt. He
found himself increasingly mourning the loss of Azeed,
both the brother he had never really known when they were
young and the brother who had now cut him out of his life.
He was also all too aware that he hadn't been able to fulfil
his mother's dying wish, either, and that lay heavily in his
heart. But how was he supposed to make her peace with
Azeed if Azeed refused to have anything to do with him?

'But I actually meant the price of giving up the life I had
made for myself. Giving up everything I had worked for.'

He knew from the beat of silence that Nadia was ready
to pounce again.

'Is that not a small sacrifice to pay?'

'No, not so small, actually.' Irritation prickled his skin.
He was *not* going to let Nadia belittle him. 'I have built
up an extremely successful business facilitating numerous multibillion-dollar takeovers over the years. That's not
something that just happens, you know. That takes hard
work and determination. It takes investment, and by that
I mean commitment and energy. I am very proud of what
I have achieved.'

'I'm sure.' Nadia's small words, along with the briefly raised brows, perfectly conveyed just what she thought of his achievements. Which only served to turn up the heat in Zayed's blood even more. Somehow she always managed to do this to him, to creep under his defences to make him justify himself. To make him *care*. 'But now you have the greater pride of being the sheikh of Gazbiyaa.'

'Yes.' Zayed put his knife and fork together and touched his napkin to his lips. 'Yes, I do.' With a sigh of frustration he realised he was never going to convince Nadia that his past life had any worth—he might as well give up now. In fact, he had no idea why he was persevering. He certainly wasn't going to tell her that pride had been the last thing he'd felt when he'd discovered he was to be crowned sheikh of Gazbiyaa. Shock, disbelief, horror even, had all ranked much higher on his list of emotions.

If he was honest, he knew he was still struggling to come to terms with the enormous change to his life, the crushing weight of the crown. His duty to his country was absolute, his commitment without question, but it was a duty and commitment that threatened to drain his spirit, eat into his soul.

And his marriage to Nadia had only made things a hundred times worse, turning a difficult situation into one that was almost intolerable. If he had inherited a simmering cauldron of oil, she had gone and chucked a bucket of water into it. Which now left him hissing with frustration.

Faced with his fury, Zayed had to admit that it wasn't just their marriage and its possible repercussions that fired him up, although that was bad enough. More worryingly, it was the presence of Nadia herself. The person she was, the way she affected him, the conflicting reactions she provoked. There was bitterness for the way she had deceived him; anger, too, for letting himself be fooled by her. Then there was the enormous sense of responsibility he felt for her and, even though that shocked him with its primeval strength, that was nothing compared to his most shocking reaction of all. Desire. Or to put it another way, the gut-wrenching, fly-busting, all-consuming lust. Which he was finding harder and harder to conceal from her and deny to himself. But that didn't mean he would stop trying. He hardened his voice.

'But along with the pride of being crowned the sheikh comes a loss of freedom.' He tapped the table impatiently. 'That's all I'm saying.'

'Freedom?' Nadia repeated the word, her nose wrinkling with scorn. 'You are lucky to have ever had it to lose.'

He was about to come back with a stinging reply but then stopped in his tracks. Was that true? Was the reason he couldn't get Nadia to understand his frustration because freedom was something she had never experienced? The stark realisation pulled him up sharply.

'So I take it growing up in Harith was very constricting?' He regarded her speculatively.

'Ha!' Nadia's reply was heartfelt. 'That's one word for it. You have no idea just how constricting.'

'Well, tell me, then.' Zayed leaned back in his chair, crossing one long leg over the other, deliberately swinging the spotlight in her direction. 'Tell me what it was like.'

'It was stifling, suffocating, insulting.' The strength of her feeling swelled the breath in Nadia's chest, pushing her breasts against the fine silk fabric of her blouse. 'My life was never my own at all. I was just an appendage, a frippery, something to be dressed up and displayed as an object. As a woman I was never allowed to have an opinion of my own and as the only daughter of the sheikh of Harith I was expected to do as I was told, to obey orders unquestioningly.'

Zayed could certainly see that would be a problem in

Nadia's case. 'What about your brother? Did you not form a relationship with him?'

'Imran? No, absolutely not. He is his father's son. Too weak to have a mind of his own or too stupid to even re-alise that he needs one. When he becomes sheikh of Harith I fear for the people of the kingdom even more.'

'And you were expected to take orders from him, too?' Zayed probed further.

'Yes, of course. I had to. And he took great pleasure in dishing out the punishments. But the more they tried to tighten the straps on the straitjacket, the more determined I was that I was going to break free. I didn't deliberately want to cause trouble, but I knew that I would never let my-self end up like my mother, as much as I love her, with all the spirit drained from her by the overbearing men in her life.'

Zayed stared at the flushed cheeks and sparkling eyes of the young woman opposite him. She had pushed her half-eaten plate of food away from her, as if the memory of her past life had taken away her appetite, and she now stubbornly held his gaze, involuntarily blinking her dark lashes at him.

Suddenly he realised that he had been so caught up in his own life, so furious with the way he had been duped by her, that he had hardly spared a thought for her feel-ings, for the life she had been so desperate to escape from and the life she now found herself imprisoned in. Was that how Nadia saw him, as just another overbearing man in her life?

He looked down at her delicate hands, the left one, com-plete with the gold band that he had slid onto her third finger, resting on the table in front of her, the other one clasping her wrist. He had felt those hands skim over his body, his skin tightening and stiffening beneath her touch. He had felt those hands circle his shaft, tentatively feel its weight before stroking the length of him with such a sensitive caress that he had let out a mew like a strangled cat; only the intense pleasure of looking at her face as she had done it stopping him from climaxing there and then, as if the overload of sensual delirium had scrambled his poor brain, leaving it not knowing what to do for the best.

'So—' Zayed shifted in his seat, determined to focus on something other than the stirring in his pants '—when your betrothal was arranged, that was when you knew you had to leave?'

'Yes. Otherwise I would have been trapped forever.'

'You fled from the oppression of your life in Harith only to end up in the very heart of your country's most bitter enemy. Hardly a sensible decision, if you don't mind my saying, if you were looking for your freedom.'

'I wasn't looking for freedom.' Nadia glared at him, eyes flashing. 'I was looking to make a difference. That's what I keep trying to tell you. I was looking for a way to stop my country from going to war. That's why I came to Gazbiyaa.'

If Zayed had had any lingering doubts about the truth of Nadia's claims they were well and truly dispelled now. Her passion and conviction shimmered around her like an aura, lighting up her whole body. There was no doubt that she was genuine, that she had come here to do what she thought was right.

Perhaps it wasn't surprising that she was so hostile towards him, why she took a swipe at him every opportunity she got. It pained Zayed to admit it, but he could see why he irritated her so much. Nadia had risked everything to be here—risked her life, in fact. Whereas he was here under sufferance, still mourning the life he had left. They had ended up in the same place with the same goals, but one had fought to get here and the other was resentful of it. Suddenly he felt humbled. Maybe he should have accepted the role he now had, the title of sheikh of Gazbi-yaa, with more grace, more gratitude. Maybe he should let Nadia in, at least give her a chance.

'In that case I can only commend your selflessness and bravery.' He had meant it as a compliment. Nadia had to be the bravest person he had ever met; her spirit and fire all part of what made her so damned attractive. But it seemed as if Nadia didn't take compliments from him any better than anything else. Far from softening towards him, she had pushed back her shoulders ready for a fight.

'It's not selfless or brave. I see it as a privilege to be able to help my country. Unlike you.'

*Unlike you.* There she went again. A muscle twitched in Zayed's jaw. If he had been starting to weaken, to see things from her point of view, then her contemptuous attitude had sharply brought him back to his senses. Forget selfless and brave—how about pig-headed and downright sanctimonious? His rational brain was telling him to let it go, that it really didn't matter what this infuriating woman thought of him. But his irrational brain and the rest of his hopping-mad body were itching to give her a taste of her own medicine.

'*Unlike you* I don't feel it necessary to play the martyr. We all know your sacrifice knows no bounds. You really don't need to keep shouting it from the rooftops. But perhaps I need to point out that you are not the only one making sacrifices—and before you start, I am not talking about the sacrifice of my previous life. I'm talking about being married to you. Quite frankly, that feels like the biggest sacrifice of all.'

He watched Nadia's eyes widen with a flash of something that looked like hurt before quickly narrowing again.

'Well, that goes for me too.' She tossed back her head with such vehement disdain that the bouncing black curls of her hair positively shone with it. 'Because, believe me, that is the biggest sacrifice for me, too.'

'Good.' He glared back at her. 'I'm so glad we find something to agree on.'

Nadia tucked her feet up under her and looked around her. She had come out to one of her favourite hideaways, a relatively small palace courtyard with rows of columns supporting ornate arches on all four sides and cushioned benches tucked inside. A wide rill cut through the abstract pattern of the tiled floor, and now the peaceful scene was floodlit a glowing orange.

She pulled her pashmina more tightly around her shoulders. It was getting cool, the temperature dropping fast. Which was more than she could say about her own.

She didn't think hers would ever drop below boiling point as far as Zayed was concerned, tonight's dinner *conversation* simply proving that point. It seemed they were totally incapable of spending any time together without it descending into tit-for-tat arguments, squabbling over who held the moral high ground and who could hurt the other most. Well, guess what, Zayed had won that one, hands down. His final comment, that she was his biggest sacrifice of all, had sliced through her like a cold steel blade, leaving a chasm of hurt. But at least she had managed to hurl his contempt right back at him, not shown him any sign of the damage his words had done. Or, worse still, the deep-rooted weakness she had for him.

She hated herself for that weakness. It undermined her, unsettled her, made her question everything she was trying to do here. Why did his cruel words hurt so much? Leave her feeling as she did now, raw and exposed and like a fraud for caring so much. Neither of them had entered this marriage for anything other than practical reasons. How he felt about her shouldn't matter.

But it did matter. Nadia hugged her arms around herself. For some reason it seemed to matter a lot.

The ringtone of Zayed's phone had finally ended their bitter exchange, Nadia only too happy to nod her assent when Zayed had asked if she minded if he took the call, seizing it as an excuse to escape. Sweeping out of the room, she had heard him say 'Clio', followed by an easy laugh that indicated just how pleased he was to hear from his beautiful British friend, immediately relaxing in a way that he never did in her company. A pang of jealousy joined the pit of misery in her stomach. There was undoubtedly a special connection between these two; Nadia had sensed it at the wedding. But she absolutely refused to let herself think about that now. After all, Clio had just married Stefan, one quarter of the indomitable Columbia Four, one of Zayed's closest friends. There couldn't be anything more than friendship between them. Could there?

Lowering her head so that she could look beyond the archway, she stared up into the rectangle of deep blue sky, studded with early stars, hoping to find some comfort in the wider universe. Instead, the wider universe was immediately forgotten as something else caught her eye. Zayed, tall and dark, striding purposefully towards her with what looked like a laptop under his arm.

'I hope I'm not disturbing you?'

He had seated himself on the bench beside her before she'd had the chance to reply, opening the laptop while she was still untucking her legs and edging away from him. His telephone conversation seemed to have improved his mood.

'It's just that I've had an idea, something that you could help me with.'

Help him? This was a first. Despite herself, despite their earlier bitter words, Nadia felt her hopes soar. Could it be that he was going to listen to her at last, let her explain her ideas for talks between Harith and Gazbiyaa? She inched back a little closer, glancing at his shadowed profile illuminated by the screen of the laptop.

'You know I will do whatever I can to help.'

'That was Clio on the phone.' Zayed was concentrating on moving his finger over the touchpad of the laptop. 'She sends her love, by the way.'

Did she indeed? Nadia took in a breath. She had to stop this stupid grudge of jealousy. She was being ridiculous. Clio had been nothing but kind to her.

'How is she? And Stefan?'

'Yes, fine.' Distracted, Zayed offered no more information. 'Ah, here we are.' He moved to close the gap between them, turning the laptop so that she could see the screen better. She could feel his denim-covered thigh branding its warmth onto her skin. 'I don't know if I've mentioned this to you, but I am one of the founder members of a charity, The Knights of Columbia.' He turned to look at her briefly. 'That's me, Christian, Stefan and—'

'Rocco. Yes, I know.'

'I'm not sure which one of us named it but none of us is owning up to it now.' He gave a short laugh. 'Anyway, this is the website.' She could sense his pride as he leaned in closer. Sense the strength and heat of his masculine body too, now that he was so close. Just for a second she let herself savour the intimacy of the moment. The two of them side by side, in the dimly glowing light of their almost cosy recess of the courtyard.

'The success of the charity has exceeded our most idealistic dreams, but the downside of that is the pressure of keeping it all going.' He really had the most lovely voice, deep and dark and compelling. 'None of us have had much time to devote to it lately, and Clio has just reminded me that if we want to keep a healthy balance sheet we need to keep chasing the donations.'

'What is the charity for?' Clutching on to her runaway senses, she focused on asking a sensible question.

'Here, this is the mission statement.' Zayed moved the cursor. 'Basically we are funding disadvantaged youngsters who deserve a good education but don't have the money to pay for it. Educating kids out of poverty, if you like. Like I say, it's been wildly successful.'

Nadia didn't doubt it. The images of smiling young people now scrolling endlessly across the screen had to be a testament to that.

'What we need is someone to keep a track of the benefactors, remind them of the importance of the work they are supporting, make sure they are spreading the word, that sort of thing. We employ a small team of people and Clio has taken on the role of finance director, which is fantastic, but she could do with some help. Basically these philanthropists appreciate the personal touch. Direct contact from one of the Knights seems to be the fastest way to get them to open their wallets.'

'But I am only the wife of a Knight.' Nadia slanted him a doubtful look. 'Will that count?'

'Hmm, probably not.' If she had been hoping for confirmation of the importance of her role, Zayed's pondering reply had squashed it flat. No doubt *Clio* was influential enough in her own right. Zayed's eyes held hers for a second; deep, dark and sexy eyes that managed to draw her in and push her away at the same time, like opposing poles of a magnet. 'I think it would be best if you sent the emails in my name. After I've okayed them, of course.'

'Of course.' Nadia tried her hardest to bite back the sarcasm. She didn't know whether to be flattered or insulted. Her initial hopes had done a spiralling nosedive when she had found out the sort of help he was talking about. But at least he was letting her into one small part of his life and that had to be better than nothing. If she could gain his trust she might be able to find a chink in this knight's impenetrable armour.

'So what do you think?' Closing the laptop, Zayed held it out in front of her. 'Will you do it?'

'Yes, I'd be glad to.' She congratulated herself on her sunny acceptance as she took the laptop from him.

'Thank you. That will be a great help.' Zayed rose to his feet, business concluded. 'We should go inside now. It's getting cold.' He held out a hand to her, leaving her no choice but to take it, silently waiting while she rearranged her pashmina and awkwardly tucked the laptop under her arm before finally giving her hand to him.

'I was right.' He rubbed her fingers with his own. 'You are cold. Let's go in.'

'I'm fine.' Nadia hastily reclaimed the offending hand but still found herself crossing the courtyard with Zayed and together they went back into the palace. The bright lights of the entrance hall made her blink.

'Right, I'd better get back to work, then.' Closing the door behind them, Zayed turned to look down at her.

'Yes, me, too.' Nadia jiggled the laptop under her arm. 'Thanks again for this.'

'You're welcome.'

They stared at each other for a long, awkward moment.

'Let me know if you need any help.' Zayed's husky, sexy voice, combined with the dark knowing look in his eyes, sent a shiver of arousal tiptoeing down Nadia's spine.

'I will.'

'Or better still…'

'Yes?'

'Just ask Clio. She's brilliant.'

Nadia looked at the time displayed in the corner of the screen: 23:35. She had been working on this laptop for several hours, propped up on the bed with a pile of pillows behind her. As she'd never had her own computer, her brother expressly forbidding it, her lack of IT skills had slowed her down, but now her research was done and she stretched back her shoulders and flexed her cramped fingers. She had her list of contacts ready to email, but that was a job for tomorrow.

She was impressed, seriously impressed, with The Knights of Columbia charity. It was obvious that these four highly successful friends had done an astoundingly good job, offering young people from all over the world an education to transform their lives and the lives of their families. But that came at a huge financial cost. Which made her all the more determined to do her job well and get those donations rolling in.

She was just about to close the laptop when she decided to look into the email situation. She would need to be able to access Zayed's email if she was to contact these benefactors in his name. She wasn't going to tell Zayed, but she had never actually sent an email before. But how hard could it be? She clicked on the envelope icon. Easy, she was straight in, no password needed. An inbox full of messages faced her. Well, she certainly wasn't going to look at those. She had no desire to torture herself with anything she might find there, and besides that was snooping.

She moved the cursor looking for how to send a message and found herself inadvertently clicking on Sent Mail. No, that wasn't right. She was just about to move on when a name jumped out at her. Azeed Al Afzal. Nadia hesitated. She shouldn't look, she knew she shouldn't, but maybe if it was only a very quick peek? Suddenly temptation had pressed her finger before her more honourable brain could stop it, and she found herself staring at a string of messages from Zayed to his brother, each one colder and more blunt than the one before. They started with Zayed encouraging Azeed to contact him, and they finally petered out with a terse, 'Whenever you are ready to talk to me, I will be here.' Not one of them had received a reply.

Nadia stared at the messages. Okay, she knew she shouldn't have read them, but now that she had maybe she could help. She was certainly sure she could be more persuasive than that. If she could get Azeed to contact Zayed, and if Azeed really was in Harith as Hassan Rouhani had suggested, maybe he could facilitate some sort of meeting with her father and brother. It was worth a try.

With her fingers hovering over the keyboard, she bit down hard on her lip, concentrating on how best to phrase this. Right, she was ready. She lowered her fingers.

Dear Azeed,
I appeal to you today as my only brother...

# CHAPTER NINE

IT WAS THE falcon soaring overhead that eventually gave away Zayed's whereabouts, majestically cutting through the early-morning pale blue sky to land on his master's outstretched arm.

By the time Nadia had reached them they were back at the weathering yard, the area where these pampered, highly trained killers spent their days. Nadia didn't like these birds any more than they looked as if they liked her. Their sharp beaks and even sharper eyes made her decidedly nervous.

But the sight of Zayed with this falcon on his arm sent her heart rate, already beating fast from the exertion of hurrying here, whirring into overdrive. Wearing jeans and a thick grey sweater, he stood tall and majestic, looking even more dashingly handsome than usual in this rural setting, the bird perched on the worn leather gauntlet on his arm.

They both turned in her direction as she cautiously approached. Neither of them looked pleased to see her.

Nadia steadied herself. The excitement of her errand was tinged with more than a little anxiety of how Zayed would receive it.

She had woken early that morning, the realisation of what she had done the night before, rashly sending that email to Azeed, making her reach across for the laptop on her bedside table. She hadn't supposed Azeed would reply. She would delete her message, then Zayed would never know what she had done.

But with a gasping intake of breath she'd realised she was wrong. For it had been there—a reply from Azeed Al Afzal. Impatiently pushing the tangled curls away from her face, she had clicked on the email with a shaking hand, her eyes darting over the message. And what she had seen was even better, more exciting than she could have hoped for.

Now Nadia just had to let Zayed know the good news.

'Hello there,' she started breezily.

'What are you doing here?' It wasn't an auspicious start, Zayed obviously not in the mood for pleasantries.

'I just thought I would come and find you.' Nadia stopped in front of them, gulping down a dry breath, her chest rising and falling rapidly. 'To tell you that you have a message.'

'A message?'

'Yes.' She forced herself to look into his eyes. 'An email. From Azeed.'

'Azeed?' A mixture of shock and hope crossed his face, twisting something deep inside her. The falcon ruffled its feathers.

'I was checking the emails this morning, for the charity work, I mean, and I just happened to notice it.' Nadia's rehearsed speech tangled round her tongue, the piercing stares of both Zayed and the creature sitting on his arm proving difficult to ignore. 'I thought you would like to know straight away.'

'Yes, thank you.' His words held a caution now, as did his eyes, boring into her, questioning, suspicious. Nadia braced herself, waiting for the interrogation.

'This email, when did it arrive?'

'Um, early this morning, I think.'

'Early this morning.' He repeated her answer, his eyes never leaving her face. 'So it just happened to arrive when you were in possession of my laptop?'

'Yes.' Nadia's casual reply wasn't fooling either of them, as Zayed's narrow-eyed stare clearly proved.

'How very fortuitous.'

'Well, actually—'

'Save it.' His voice harsh now, Zayed's jaw clenched before he turned away from her, moving to transfer the reluctant bird onto one of the circular perches behind them. 'I'll see you back in the palace in ten minutes.'

Nadia hesitated. She was going to have to tell him what she'd done. But maybe she would wait until they were inside. Until they were well away from that bird.


'Just what is the meaning of this?'

They were in Zayed's office, the laptop open on the table in front of them, Azeed's email filling the screen.

Nadia had waltzed in, bearing the laptop before her like some sort of prize, a swirl of floral scents, colt-like limbs and unconsciously sexy movements. Now she stood beside him as he sat glaring at the screen, breathing lightly as she looked over his shoulder, seemingly determined to mess with his self-control.

She was still wearing the skinny jeans she'd had on earlier, but now the jacket had gone, revealing a loose-fitting, sleeveless pink top. Somehow, on Nadia, it managed to be one of the sexiest outfits he had ever seen.

He had been out flying Kali, his favourite falcon, when he had spotted her in the distance, purposefully making her way towards him. His heart had done an inexplicable loop at the sight of her, which he had quickly channelled into annoyance. After all, he had gone out there to briefly get away from the burdens of his life and, apart from the impending war, Nadia was the biggest burden of all.

Despite all his efforts he was no closer to solving the problem of Harith. The threat of war showed no sign of abating and all the negotiating skills that he prided himself on, skills he had employed so profitably to make his own company so successful, counted for nothing when dealing with a country like Harith. It seemed as if war was the only language they understood.

He was no closer to solving the problem of Nadia, either. Or, more specifically, the infuriating attraction he felt for her. He had been so determined that this deceitful, duplicitous young woman would be a wife in name only, that no way in the world would he let himself be tempted to take her to his bed.

That first day, when she had told him who she really was, he had been sure that would be easy. His anger had totally consumed him, overpowering everything, even managing to blot out the heated sexual attraction between them, along with the feverish memory of the night they had just spent together. In an effort to claw back control he had convinced himself that this woman was anathema to him.

But time had taken that anathema, that seething anger, and turned it to molten rock. It was still there in the pit of his stomach, making its weight felt whenever he thought of the way she had lied to him. But time had done something else, too. It had curled round his defences, twisting insidiously inside him, tightening its traitorous hold.

For with each passing day his yearning for this totally impossible woman grew and grew. To the point where she only had to enter the room for his heart rate to ramp up to an alarming level, only had to be within six feet of him for the ache in his groin to start up.

It was in danger of driving him completely crazy. Especially when she insisted on meddling in his affairs. Especially when she damned well went and did things like emailing his brother behind his back.

'Well, if you would just let me explain...'

'Please do.' Zayed leaned back in his chair, pushing it farther away from the desk, away from her, affecting a cool nonchalance that fooled neither of them. He was just about managing to control his anger, but they both knew it was there, simmering beneath the forced politeness.

'I was working on the computer and I just happened to come across your emails to your brother, and I could see that you hadn't been able to persuade him to reply to you and—'

'So you read my personal emails?'

'Not all of them. Not any of them except the ones to your brother.'

'Oh, that's all right, then.'

'Anyway—' Nadia dodged past the boulder of his sarcasm '—when I saw what you'd written I wasn't surprised that Azeed hadn't been persuaded to answer—'

'Stop right there.' Zayed sat bolt upright again. 'Not only do you read my private emails but then you have the audacity to stand there and tell me what is wrong with them?'

'Well, someone had to,' Nadia fought back. 'Because they were all wrong, Zayed. There was no emotion in them, nothing that sounded as if it came from the heart. You approached your brother as if he was just another business deal that you were trying to wrap up, that his disappearance was a mildly irritating mystery rather than something that actually meant anything to you.'

'I did no such thing. That is *not* true. How dare you tell me how to speak to my brother when you have never even met the man? You know absolutely nothing about him.'

'And neither do you, by the sound of it.'

The arrow of Nadia's reply pierced his shield of anger and for a moment he could only glare at her. Was she right? Did he really not know his brother at all?

'Anyway—' she tossed back her head, using his silence to her advantage '—I knew I could do a better job.'

'Did you indeed? So you took it upon yourself to email

*my* brother—' he turned back to the laptop, scrolling down to Nadia's message '—this schmaltzy piece of fiction, in *my* name, without telling *me*?'

'Yes, yes, I did. Because if I had asked you, you would never have let me do it.'

'Too damned right I wouldn't. You had absolutely no right to do this.'

'But the point is, it worked, Zayed. You might call it schmaltzy, but Azeed saw it for what it was. A message from the heart.'

'Your heart, Nadia. Not mine.'

Nadia gave him the full force of her glittering eyes. 'Maybe that's because you don't know where to find yours.'

Zayed knew exactly where his heart was. He could feel it trying to fight its way out of his rib cage. Outrage at what Nadia had done, anger that she dared to challenge him in this way, combined with a horrible sneaking feeling that she might possibly have a valid point, had it bucking like a rodeo horse in his chest.

'Look.' She took a step closer, gesturing to the laptop screen. He caught the warm, lemony scent of the curtain of hair that swung across one side of her face before she tucked it behind her ear. 'You may not approve of my methods—' she waited for his snort of understatement to die away '—but thanks to my message, not only are you in contact with your brother again but he is agreeing to help arrange a meeting with my family.'

And that was what this was all about, wasn't it? Nadia's sole focus. He could see her face alight with excitement, hear the hope and optimism shining in her voice. This was what the whole charade of their marriage had been set up for, to try to find a way to secure peace.

He ran a hand over his brow, leaving it across his eyes while he collected his thoughts. Wanting to save her country from the horrors of going to war with Gazbiyaa was the most noble of ambitions. It was what he wanted, too, more than anything. So why did it irritate the hell out of him? Why did it *hurt*?

'I suppose you think you have been very clever?' He lowered his voice, the dark, mocking tone he had been aiming for somehow sounding more like petulance.

'No, not clever.' She had moved closer to him again, too close. 'I just want to try to find a way forward, Zayed, that's all. The same as you do.'

'Okay, fine.' He stood up abruptly, the chair skittering away behind him, reaching forward to close the laptop with far more force than was necessary. 'I accept that your intervention has proved successful in this instance.' *Intervention has proved successful.* Since when had he become so pompous? 'Just don't expect me to start thanking you for it.'

'I won't.' Nadia smiled sweetly at him. 'I already know that pride of yours would never let you.'

Zayed shot her a vicious stare. God, she was an infuriating, smug, self-righteous, sanctimonious piece of work. He would have liked to have put her across his knee, to pull down those jeans and expose the pale buttocks and then…maybe run his hands over the soft rounds of flesh, feel the goose bumps rising beneath his touch before sliding his fingers down between her…

'You will email your brother back, won't you?' Nadia's bossy instructions brought him coldly back to his senses. 'Right away, I mean. Make sure that he knows you want this meeting as soon as possible?'

'I'll tell you what—' Zayed growled, a new wave of bitterness temporarily numbing the sexual ache that was gripping his body '—why don't you do it for me, Nadia? I'm sure you would do a much better job.'

He watched Nadia hesitate, unsure. 'Well, if you would like me to I'd be quite happy—'

'No!' He bit back the barely contained rage. 'I would *not* like you to. *I* will email my brother what I want, when I want.'

'Yes, of course.' She turned, heading for the door, one hand jammed into the back pocket of her jeans. 'But I should do it now.' She glanced back. 'And if you want me to look over it first, before you send it…'

Zayed folded his arms over his rigid rising chest. He aimed a look at her, holding her steady in his gun sight, a look that held everything that he refused to say out loud. It scorched a pathway between them that finally succeeded in having Nadia hotfooting it from the room.

Exhaling a long breath, Zayed moved the chair back to his desk and sat down heavily. Opening the laptop, he saw Azeed's email staring back at him. He would read it again now, slowly this time, without the anger blurring his vision.

Dearest brother,
I thank you for sparing the time to contact me during what must be a period of great turbulence and anxiety for you.

He was certainly right about that. Zayed read on.

My heart goes out to you as I now know that yours does to me. I am humbled by your conciliatory words and beg your forgiveness for my silence.

He leaned his elbows on the desk, covering his nose and mouth with his cupped hands. Suddenly he wanted a drink—and it was still barely 10:00 a.m.

It was born of an anger that should never have encompassed you, an anger that was aimed at my father and my changed circumstances. Futile, of course, but I hope you will understand.

But now your generosity of spirit has made me see it is time to move forward. I will gladly do all I can to help facilitate a meeting between you and the sheikh, as you have requested. It will be a relief to be able to use the newly discovered Harithian blood in my veins to some good.
Your loving brother
Azeed

Zayed looked away from the screen, running a hand over the top of his head, guilt and shame coursing through him.

Guilt that he had never valued his brother for the man he was, never tried to get to know him. And shame that he had always been too busy with his own life, making his first million, chasing the next deal and bedding a string of beautiful women along the way, to even realise it.

It wasn't as if he didn't value friendship. He would have laid down his life for his three sworn blood brothers, Stefan, Christian and Rocco. *The Columbia Four.* The bond between them was unbreakable, despite the unexpected pressures that had been put on them this year. But what about his real brother, his true blood brother? At least, the 50 per cent of it from their father. What had he ever done for him?

I am humbled by your conciliatory words. If anyone was humbled it was him. Humbled by the way Azeed had taken the crumbs of comfort of Nadia's words and gobbled them up like a starving beast. Nadia had been right. He *had* approached Azeed in totally the wrong way.

And the dire situation with Harith? Had he approached that the wrong way, too? Was Nadia right about that, as well?

Zayed got up from his chair and strode over to the window, placing the flat of his palms against the glass as he gazed across the skyscape of the scorching city, at the people scurrying around far below. His people. His city. His kingdom.

This could be his chance to put things right. To make peace with his brother and maybe even find peace for his country. One thing was for sure: he was going to give it a damned good try.

Removing his hands from the window, he watched his palm prints fade away. Suddenly he knew what he had to do. He had to confide in Azeed, tell him about Nadia, exactly who this new wife of his was, none other than the daughter of the sheikh of Harith. Something he hadn't told a soul—not even his three most trusted friends.

If Azeed was going to contact Sheikh Amani on his behalf, he deserved to know the truth; he *had* to know the truth. His brother had been subjected to too many lies. His whole life had been a lie. Now it was time for the lies to stop.

But there was still one falsehood he was going to conceal. The fact that his marriage was a sham. He would tell his brother that Nadia was an Harithian princess but not that she had tricked him into the marriage, that it was a marriage in name only. His pride could only take so much of a battering.

Besides, once he was sure that relations between Gazbiyaa and Harith were sufficiently stable, he and Nadia would divorce and that would be the end of this whole horrendous debacle. There was no reason for the truth to ever come out. The thought of which should have raised his spirits, but instead left him with a hollow emptiness inside.

Because Nadia, this deceitful, conniving young woman, who taunted and riled him, who tested the limits of his patience and self-control beyond any endurance, had somehow managed to bury herself beneath his skin, lodge herself somewhere so deep inside him that he knew he would never be rid of her. He would never be rid of the craving ache of hunger for her that was now his constant companion.

It wasn't just the sexual need, although there was no doubt about that. His body had long since abandoned all subtlety where Nadia was concerned, leaping to attention, screaming *for* attention, so desperate for her that its urgency frightened him with its power.

But there was more than that, something more complex, more dangerous. Something that was just her, the essence of Nadia. If he could bottle it he would have a potion capable of mass destruction of the heart.

Nadia challenged him, confronted him and made him question everything about himself. But the biggest question was, how would he ever be able to let her go?

# CHAPTER TEN

AFTER HOURS OF nothing but the uncompromising beauty of the desert for company, and dusk fast approaching, Nadia was relieved to see the brown tented roofs of a small settlement coming into view. The journey had been long and uncomfortable, but it finally looked as if they had almost reached their destination.

'Is that it?' She pointed into the distance, worried that if she took her eyes off the encampment it might disappear like a mirage.

'Yep.' Zayed narrowed his eyes to follow her gaze, his hands gripping the steering wheel. 'We've made good time.'

They had been travelling for most of the day, Zayed rattling this six-wheeled SUV at considerable speed along the mile-wide dried-up riverbeds, following tracks around the base of the towering sandstone cliffs or negotiating a route through the psychedelic patterns of the shifting sand dunes.

The conversation had been sparse, painful even. If Nadia had hoped that this momentous thing they were doing, this shared adventure, would forge a bond between them, kindle some intimacy between them, she had been sadly disappointed. She longed to talk to him, to be able to discuss everything that was going around in her head, that she was sure was going around in his head too.

But her earlier attempts to get him to open up had failed miserably, his harsh profile making it clear that he was

concentrating on the driving, that her questions and specu-
lations were nothing but an irritating distraction. A water
bottle passed between them was as intimate as it had gotten.

So instead she had lost herself in her thoughts, gazing
out of the window at the awesome vastness of the desert, clinging on to her seat as the vehicle had leaped and
bumped over the inhospitable terrain, occasionally distracted by the odd camel train that would appear through
the clouds of dust they were throwing up. Confirmation,
at least, that they weren't the only living creatures in this
wilderness.

Nadia could still hardly believe what they were doing.
True to his word, Azeed had succeeded in setting up a
meeting at the palace of Harith, but it was with her brother,
Imran, rather than with her father. Imran had made it quite
clear that the sheikh, who was away on business, was to
know nothing about it. That he would never have agreed
to allow them into the country, let alone meet with them.

Now they were actually here in the kingdom of Harith,
albeit several hours' drive away from the palace she had
grown up in. They were going to spend tonight with Azeed
at his encampment before setting off to meet with her
brother tomorrow.

Nadia's emotions had been seesawing up and down ever
since Zayed had told her of the plans. Initially euphoric
that her subterfuge had worked, she had then braced herself for a fight, convinced that Zayed would say he was
going alone, that she had to stay in Gazbiyaa. But to her
excitement and surprise he had curtly informed her that she
would be accompanying him. More than that, she would
sit beside him at the meeting as his wife, the sheikha of
Gazbiyaa. Because he intended to tell her family the truth.
It was time to get everything out in the open.

Secretly the thought terrified her. Numbed her to the

core with its daring. But something about Zayed's calm authority had steadied her nerve, made her put her trust in him. It was clear that he had made up his mind, that nothing would sway him. So Nadia had embraced his decision without any argument, hiding her fear behind genuine eagerness and enthusiasm. *Finally* they were in this together.

With a wide spray of sand the car skidded to a halt in front of the collection of tents and Zayed jumped out, stretching back his shoulders and looking around him.

A tall, upright man emerged from the largest tent. Nadia held her breath, fascinated as she peered through the sand-speckled window of the car at the meeting of the two handsome brothers.

For a moment they stared at one another, both standing tall and proud, only a few small yards apart in distance but an ocean of mistrust and uncertainty born of their father's mistakes still separating them. Nadia watched, her heart in her throat, as Zayed, chest back and head high, held out his hand to his brother. An inexplicable stab of pride pierced her heart at the sight of this noble gesture. Silently she found herself willing, praying that Azeed would accept the handshake of reconciliation.

But she needn't have worried. For not only did Azeed take his brother's hand, but he gripped it in both of his and then the two of them were embracing, their arms locked around each other's shoulders, their hands splayed across each other's backs. Nadia hurriedly brushed away the tear that was sliding down her dusty cheek.

The brothers pulled apart and both looked in her direction, Zayed striding over to open the door and help Nadia out.

'Azeed, please allow me to introduce my wife, Nadia. Nadia, my brother, Azeed.'

The formal introduction seemed somehow fitting, as the three of them stood solemnly in the orange glow of

the desert sunset. *My wife.* For a second Nadia let herself
hold those words to her heart. Here, away from the palace,
she was not the pampered, protected sheikha—she was
just Zayed's wife. And it felt right, true. Except of course
it wasn't. She was a wife in name only, to be dispensed
with as soon as it was safe to do so. A fact that she had to
brutally remind herself of.

'I am delighted to meet you.' Azeed took her hand and
bowed his head. Wearing the traditional white dishdasha
and keffiyeh headdress, he seemed very much at home
in the beautiful but bleak wilderness of this desert. 'Welcome to my humble dwelling.' As he raised his eyes to
hers Nadia was struck by the similarity between the two
brothers, but Azeed's features were harder, sharper, more
bleak. 'I'm sure you must be very tired and hungry after
your long journey. If you would like to use the washing
facilities, a meal will be ready for you shortly.'

Humble it might have been, but the small encampment
had everything needed for a comfortable life in the desert.
From what Nadia could make out there appeared to be four
tents: a small one for ablutions, two others, presumably
for the servants or sleeping quarters, and then the larger
one, where Zayed and Azeed were now waiting for her.

But first she took a moment to look around her, to drink
in the incredible scene. She could well see why Azeed had
walked away from his complicated life in favour of this.
The last of the light was disappearing behind the dunes,
picking up the sparse patches of scrubby vegetation and
rewarding them with long, long shadows across the rusty,
orange, golden glow of the vast expanse of the wadi. And
above them a billion stars were bursting through the sky.

Zayed and Azeed were seated on rugs outside the main
tent, now festooned with flickering candles, talking quietly, but as she approached they both stopped and got to
their feet.

'Come and join us.' Azeed moved to one side so that Nadia could sit on one of the cushions between them. 'Let's eat.' He gestured to the array of dishes spread out on the mat in front of them and passed around plates. 'We have much to discuss, but first you need sustenance.'

Cautiously accepting Zayed's hand, Nadia sat down, doing her best to ignore the jolt of awareness from his touch. But seated on the tribal rugs between these two strong, dark men, she began to relax. She hadn't known how Azeed would accept her, panicking when Zayed had told her he had shared their secret with him, that she was formally Princess Nadia of Harith. But Azeed appeared to bear her no ill will and the relief was palpable that, for once, she didn't have to pretend to be someone else.

As the night wore on the conversation flowed surprisingly easily. The food was delicious, too, and eating it the traditional way with their hands only made it taste better. Sensing that there was a lot of unfinished business between the two brothers, Nadia sat back and let them talk to each other without interruption from her. It was so good to see them communicating, getting to know each other, the changed people they had become. Especially as she had been the one to bring about this meeting, even if it had been a bit underhanded.

She was surprised, and silently thrilled, how openly Azeed was prepared to confide in his brother. And when Zayed told him about their mother's dying wish, describing how she had asked him to explain to Azeed just why she had spoken out and to be sure to tell him that she had always loved him like a son, he was visibly touched.

In a softly spoken voice Azeed freely admitted that he was no longer the same man he had been. The ruthless heir apparent who would have stopped at nothing to further the expansion of his kingdom had gone, along with the embittered son who had wanted vengeance on his deceitful father. And he stressed that he no longer felt any resentment for the brother who had 'stolen' his crown.

'You do believe me when I say that, Zayed?' He fixed his brother with a penetrating stare. 'I want you to know that I bear you no ill will.'

'Of course I believe you,' Zayed replied solemnly. 'And I thank you for your honesty and for your tolerance.'

'No.' Deeply serious now, Azeed continued, 'It is I who should be thanking you. I have had a lot of time to think recently, and I see now that I was never the right person to rule Gazbiyaa. You are far better equipped for that role. I was so consumed with turning the kingdom into a global superpower that I was in danger of threatening its stability, even leading its young men into war. Believe it or not, I am grateful to have had that burden lifted from me. And very thankful that the future of Gazbiyaa is now in your capable hands.'

'Then, why not come back? You might not be the sheikh, but your help would be invaluable to me.'

'No.' Azeed slowly shook his head. 'I have my freedom now, Zayed, something I have never had before. The freedom that was once yours has been handed over to me. I see that now and I intend to use it wisely.'

'Then, make sure that you do.' Reaching across, Zayed laid a hand on his brother's shoulder. 'As my friends and I used to say, *memento vivere*—remember to live!'

'*Memento vivere...*' Azeed repeated. 'I will embrace your motto!'

The meal now finished, Azeed turned to Nadia, shadows hollowing his cheeks. 'And you, Nadia, I hope you forgive me for not attending your wedding. I'm afraid I was in a dark place then.'

'Of course.' Nadia used the excuse of washing her hand in the finger bowl to avoid Azeed's direct gaze. It had been a long day, followed by the high emotions of the evening, and she could feel a lump growing in her throat with Azeed's heartfelt words. 'You don't need to apologise. You have had so much to contend with.'

'As indeed we all have.' He glanced back at Zayed. 'But now I am so glad we are looking to the future. I think we should make a toast.'

Clapping his hands, he summoned two smiling servants who quickly cleared away the food, returning with a final tray of drinks before disappearing back into the black of the night.

Nadia watched as Azeed poured water into the three glasses, the clear liquid turning cloudy. 'Nadia, you will have a glass of arrack?'

'Um...' Nadia hesitated. She didn't actually drink alcohol, had never had so much as a sip when Zayed had a glass of wine with their evening meal. But she so much wanted to be a part of this toast, part of this team, the three of them out here under the stars, preparing for the challenge of tomorrow.

'Thank you, I think I will.'

She watched Zayed's eyes narrow as she reached forward to take the glass, and that made her all the more determined. It wasn't up to him to tell her what she could do.

'To the future and to peace.' They all clinked their glasses and Nadia took a defiant swallow. Mmm, yummy... Warm and aniseedy— In fact, more than warm—burning as it scorched down her throat and temporarily stole her breath away. Perhaps she'd be a bit more cautious with the next sip.

'And to Nadia and Zayed.' Azeed raised his glass again. 'To a long and very happy marriage.'

Their glasses clinked again, but this time they had a hollow ring. As Nadia met her husband's dark eyes something passed between them, something intense, meaningful, sad.

Ignoring her own advice, she hastily took another swallow of alcohol, leaving her gulping and gasping for air, her eyelids batting against her watering eyes. Zayed continued to stare at her, merely tipping his head slightly to one side, raising his eyebrows just a fraction before finally turning back to his brother.

'How long to reach the Amani palace tomorrow, would you say?'

'If you leave at dawn tomorrow you should be there by noon. Especially in that beast of a vehicle of yours, Zayed.' Azeed nodded his head towards the black night where the six-by-six was stabled alongside the two Arab stallions and several camels.

'Yeah, I have to say it does fly over the dunes.'

Nadia watched the two of them over the rim of her glass before trying another delicate sip. She rather liked this drink now she had gotten the hang of it. And she loved to see the relationship building between these two men.

'And you are sure you don't want me to come with you, Zayed? You know that I would be willing. Although I am afraid I would be able to offer you no protection. My dubious birthright and the fact that I live here in Harith were enough to set up a meeting with Imran Amani, but that will not guarantee your safety.'

'I understand. And I greatly appreciate all that you have done for me. But from now on this is down to me.' The determination in Zayed's voice left no room for argument.

'But you will have some security with you? In case something goes wrong?'

'Yes. I've got a small undercover team there already, checking things out, plus a couple of bodyguards if we need them. But I'm hoping we won't. I have to protect Nadia, obviously, but the aim is to show that we are looking for a peaceful solution rather than any display of strength.'

Azeed nodded his understanding, but his brow was still furrowed. 'Don't forget that the sheikh knows nothing of this meeting. According to his son there is no way he would have you on Harithian soil, let alone agree to meet with you.'

'Then I will just have to make Imran Amani see sense and hope he can get the message through to his father.'

'And you are sure that you want to tell Amani that you are married to his sister? It's a high-risk strategy. Wouldn't it be better to wait until you have made some progress with the peace negotiations before you own up to that?'

'I am sure.' Zayed met his brother's concerned eyes. 'There can be no more lies, Azeed. Our father's lies have brought us to the brink of war, and by covering up my marriage to Nadia I have simply exacerbated the threat. I see that now. The longer our secret is kept, the worse it will be when it eventually becomes known. Now is the time for truth.'

'Then, I wish you luck, brother, and I salute your bravery. Yours and Nadia's.'

Both men looked across at Nadia, who had gone strangely quiet.

She was leaning back against the cushions with her legs neatly tucked under her. But her head was lolling to one side, a thick strand of blue-black hair falling over her face and catching on her slightly parted lips, vibrating with each sleeping breath.

'I see it is time you took your wife to bed.' With a rare smile Azeed rose to his feet, Zayed close behind him. 'You have a long day ahead of you tomorrow.' And with a handshake and one final embrace the two men parted company.

*Take his wife to bed.* There was nothing Zayed would like to do better, in every sense of the phrase. Alone now, with the candles in the lanterns burning low, he looked across at his sleeping beauty. She looked ridiculously peaceful, given where they were, what they were about to face tomorrow. She was such an enigma, this young

woman. Feisty and as fierce as a tiger when she needed
to be. Challenging, autocratic and living up to her title of
princess at times when things weren't going her way. But
she was the bravest person he had ever known, with the
biggest heart and the most compassion to go with it.

Who else would throw themselves into such dangerous
situations as she did, with so little regard for their own
safety? The way she had when he had first found her in
his bed. The way she was prepared to do tomorrow.

When he had told her that she would be accompanying
him to Harith, that together they would tell her brother the
truth, she hadn't even flinched. Although the way her eyes
had darkened to violet had given her away, tugging at something inside him, making him want to reach out to her, wrap
his arms around her, tell her everything would be all right.

But of course he had done no such thing. He had just
walked away and left her to her secret fear. Because that
was the man she had turned him into. The man he had
to be.

Leaning over her now, he scooped an arm under her legs
and carefully lifted her up. She felt so light, so warm and
soft as she sleepily nuzzled against his chest, murmuring
something against his ear that was totally unintelligible
but that still sent a shaft of desire through his body.

Stepping inside the tent, he waited a second for his
eyes to accustom themselves to the near dark. There was
just one mattress laid on the ground, covered with rugs
and blankets. Squatting down, he lowered Nadia onto it,
attempting to pull back the blanket with one hand while
holding on to her with the other. Sensing the movement,
Nadia helpfully raised her arms and locked them around
his neck, unbalancing him so that they both fell down
onto the mattress.

For a minute Zayed let himself stay like that, cocooned
beside her, breathing in her scent, allowing the illicit jolt

of lust to kick in unchecked. Then, raising his hands, he extracted himself from her embrace and pulled the blanket over her fully clothed body. He was about to go, to leave her to sleep, but something about the soft pout of her mouth drew him back, and he couldn't stop himself just moving the hair from her face and leaning forward to gently brush his lips over hers. They tasted of aniseed. They tasted of desire.

There was a noise from inside the tent. A sort of muffled yelp.

Zayed listened hard. He had been sitting out here for a couple of hours now, breathing in the cold blackness of the night, thinking through what had to be done tomorrow. The silence had calmed him, broken only by the occasional call of an unknown animal or the moan of a camel.

But this sound was neither of those things. There it was again, louder now. Getting to his feet, Zayed moved towards the tent and, pulling aside the tent flap, went in, impatient that he couldn't immediately see anything. He could hear a rasping of breath and it took a second to realise it was his own, accompanying the hammering of his heart.

'Nadia?' He whispered her name, able to make out the shape of her body now, stirring beneath the blankets. 'Nadia, are you okay?'

The small cry of response had him beside her in a second and he crouched down, wrapping one arm over her body and pushing the blankets away from her buried head with the other. He could feel her trembling, her whole body shaking with whatever fear was gripping her.

'Nadia, you need to wake up.' He touched her cheek with his hand and her eyes flew open, unseeing, full of terror.

'No!' Her fists appeared from beneath the tangle of blankets, punching out at him, uselessly flailing around in the air as she fought to sit up. 'Go away, get off me.'

'You are having a bad dream, Nadia.' Catching her hands in his, he pressed them to his chest, moving closer to her to prevent them from escaping. He lowered his head so that it was level with hers, speaking softly. 'That's all.'

He could see recognition slowly dawning now, the wide eyes staring back at him with dazed confusion, but the fear still there, shaking her body.

'Zayed?'

'Yes, it's me.'

'But you are so cold.' The panic was beginning to mount again, her hands trying to escape, pull themselves from his grasp, her eyes darting wildly over his face. 'Why are you so cold?'

'Because I've been outside.'

'Outside?' She stopped struggling as she tried to understand his words.

'Yes. Outside the tent. It's cold out there.'

'Oh.' She let out a shuddering breath, her eyes focusing now, steadying. 'Not because...' She faltered, confusion and embarrassment lowering her voice. 'I thought...I thought you were dead.'

'No!' Zayed laughed sharply. 'I'm definitely not dead.'

'Thank God.' With another breath that shuddered the whole length of her she leaned forward into him, lowering her head so that he was breathing into her tangled hair, the intoxicating scene filling his nostrils. 'It was terrible. Someone was coming to kill me, he had a knife, it was already covered in blood...'

'It's over, Nadia, forget about it.'

'He said it was your blood, Zayed. He said he had killed you and I was next.'

'It was just a nightmare.' Feeling her starting to shake again, Zayed released her hands and moved his own round to the back of her head, pulling her closer to him.

'Yes—' she breathed the hot words against the base of

his neck '—just a nightmare. But it was so real, Zayed.'
She shivered violently. 'The blood on the knife, the way
it had smeared right up to the hilt... You don't think...'
She tried to pull back to look into his face, but Zayed held
her firm against his chest. 'Don't think that it might be a
warning of some sort, that it holds a meaning?'

'No, Nadia, I don't. No warning, no hidden meaning,
just your body reacting to what we have to do tomorrow.
It's stress, that's all, invading your subconscious.'

He waited for her denial, sure that she wouldn't accept
that her night terrors could be the manifestation of any
sort of weakness on her part. Especially if it was being
pointed out by him. But it seemed he was wrong. Sinking down against him, Nadia burrowed her head against
his chest and in a very quiet voice he heard her say, 'I'm
frightened, Zayed. Frightened about what might happen,
that it might go terribly wrong.'

'It won't.' Moving one hand round her back, Zayed
splayed the other across her skull, threading his fingers
through her hair, gently massaging away the tension.
'Nothing is going to go wrong.' Despite her obvious dis-
tress, he felt a small surge of triumph. To have Nadia finally opening up to him, letting him see the vulnerability
beneath her normal haughty disregard, triggered a deeply
primal reaction in him. And to have her warm body nes-
tled in his arms like this, to be able to comfort her, felt
just plain good.

With her head pressed against his heart he knew she
had to be able to hear its quickening thump, but he couldn't
control it, any more than he could control the warm spread
of arousal that was now percolating through his body. In
an effort to disguise it he injected a no-nonsense burr into
his voice.

'I can handle your brother. You don't have to worry

about anything. We'll do what has to be done tomorrow and then we're out of there, straight back to Gazbiyaa.'

'But supposing…' Nadia stirred in his arms, tipping up her face to look at him, her eyes shining anxiously in the darkness of the tent. 'Supposing my brother won't let me go back with you?'

'What do you mean?' Zayed loosened his hold enough to be able to lean back to look into her face more clearly.

'I mean—' he heard her constricted swallow '—my brother might decide I have to stay in Harith to face the punishment for what I have done.'

'And you think I would let that happen?'

'I don't know. Once our secret is revealed and my family knows the truth, you no longer have to be responsible for me.'

'Is that what you *really* think?' Incredulity hardened his voice, slamming the brakes on his body's arousal. 'That I would hand you over to your brother and walk away, leave you to face whatever barbaric punishment he saw fit?'

'Possibly, yes.'

'Well, thank you for the vote of confidence, Nadia.' Anger now tainted his voice. 'I know you have always had a low opinion of me, but this is really plummeting new depths. I'm appalled that you would ever think I would treat you in such a way.'

'Well, can you blame me?' In a show of defiance Nadia arched her back to push against his arms, but her voice was cracked with anguish. 'You have never made any secret of the fact that you want to be rid of me.'

'Don't be ridiculous.'

'This could be your chance.'

'Nadia, stop!' Catching her face in his hands, Zayed held it there, his palms under her chin, his fingers framing her jawline. A physical jolt of longing kicked in again at the sight of her captured expression, the wide-eyed challenge, lips slightly parted as if frozen in mid-protest. 'I would never let anything happen to you. *Ever.* Do I make myself clear?'

For a second Nadia didn't move, just staring at him, obviously weighing up whether that could be true. Then finally she nodded, her eyelids dropping. 'Yes, thank you. I guess I'm just being stupid.' She took in a faltering breath. 'But being back here on Harithian soil… I don't know… I suppose it has affected me more than I thought.'

'I can see that. But there is no need to be frightened. No harm will come to you, Nadia. I promise you that.'

'Thank you.'

'And you don't need to keep thanking me. You are my wife after all.'

'Yes. I am, aren't I?' Nadia tilted back her head and her eyes darkened, fear now giving way to another, altogether more dangerous, response. 'Your wife.'

The words sat softly on her lips, taunting Zayed with their false simplicity. Was it deliberate, that warm, generous pout? Did she know what it did to him? What *she* did to him? Whatever else, he knew he had to fight it.

'And since you are my wife, it is obviously my duty to protect you.'

'Your duty.' Her eyes registered his veiled slight. 'Yes, of course.'

They stared at one another.

'I should go.' Zayed rocked back on his heels, intending to stand, walk away, remove himself from temptation.

'Go?'

'Yes. You need to get some more sleep.' His voice sounded gruff, distant. 'There are still a couple of hours before dawn.'

'But what about you? Have you had any sleep at all?'

He hesitated, his throat gripped by silence as he watched Nadia move to one side, start to pull at the rucked-up blankets beneath her. Surely she could see that sleep was the very last thing on his mind. 'No, not yet.'

'Then why don't you come and lie down here?' She indicated the torturously tempting rumpled space she had made on the mattress beside her.

'I don't think that would be a very good idea.'

Nadia angled her head to better look into his eyes. 'I would like you to join me.'

'Nadia…'

'Please.'

Before he had time to dodge the lure of her seduction she had reached out to touch his face, running the back of her hand down his cheek, trailing her fingers erotically across his lips.

'Please,' she repeated, whispering into the darkness between them. 'I want you to.'

How the hell was he supposed to resist that? The dam wall of his defence could take no more, caving into the flood of his desire. Catching her hand, he pressed it against his open mouth, dragging his bottom lip against her palm, raising his eyes to hers as he took her thumb and slowly sucked it into his mouth. Nadia moaned gratifyingly. She really did want him.

In case he needed any further confirmation she leaned forward, hooking her free arm around his shoulder and pulling him towards her until together they fell backwards onto the mattress. Zayed was desperate to feel her mouth against his now. That damned sensuous mouth, which had been taunting him for weeks with its perfect pout and its seductively infuriating curve that he already knew fitted so well against his own. That would fit so well against other parts of his body, too.

He rolled on top of her, claiming those plump, luscious lips, his erection pressing hard and insistent through the tangle of clothes and twisted blankets. Hot and fierce, he plundered his tongue into her open mouth, feeling Nadia surrender to the power, hearing her groan into his need. She squirmed beneath him, her hands around the back of his neck, arching her body, sealing them together, all the proof he needed that she felt this burning, reckless desire too, shared the tumult of sexual hunger.

His whole body throbbed with it, had to be satisfied, but these wretched clothes were in the way. Prising himself out of her arms, Zayed stumbled to his feet, yanking off his jeans and boxers, pulling his sweatshirt over his head, all in a matter of seconds. He looked down at Nadia, who was kneeling now, fumbling with the buttons of her shirt, still wearing the cargo pants she had travelled in. She stared back at him, her mouth falling open, her eyes glittering in the dim light at the sight of his completely naked, fully aroused body. Yes—he could do this to her. He could make her tremble with yearning for him.

The clothes had to go. He joined her and they tugged at the buttons together, pulling at her trousers until they came down with her panties still inside them, to be tossed to one side. As the cold air hit the heat of her skin a shower of goosebumps skittered over her, her nipples shrinking to hardened peaks when he unfastened her bra and set free her swollen breasts. God, she was stunning.

On top of her again, he took each nipple in his mouth in turn, his breath rasping, the hot slick of saliva cooling on her skin as he grazed his teeth against her, tugging at her until she moaned with tortured pleasure. Arching her back, she thrust her hands into his hair, clutching at handfuls of it to pull him even closer. Zayed raised his head. He could go up now, back to her lips. Or down...

Nadia threw back her head, totally, wantonly giving herself up to this man, to the exquisite way he could make her feel, to everything he could do to her. His rasping tongue had made its way down the clenching muscles of her ab-

domen and now it was between her opening legs, parting
her moist folds, sliding inside, his breath hot and damp,
his beard rough against her skin. She gasped as he found
her clitoris, tilting her pelvis up to him, desperate for him
not to stop this exquisite rubbing, stroking motion. Sensing her need, Zayed relentlessly played his tongue over
her throbbing nub, increasing the pressure until she knew
she could bear it no more and with a massive, shuddering
convulsion she tipped past the point of consciousness and
over the edge of oblivion.

Zayed gazed down at Nadia's face. She had never looked
more beautiful to him: her cheeks hot with the glow of her
orgasm, her hair all over the place, her eyes still glazed
with desire. His need for her burned like nothing he had
ever known before.

Covering her mouth with his own, he positioned himself
between her legs but he felt her twist beneath him. So she
wanted to be on top. They rolled over, Nadia bestriding
his groin, her hair tumbling wildly over her shoulders, her
hands placed firmly on his chest. She looked magnificent.
Unable to wait a moment longer, he pulled her down on
top of him and with one powerful thrust was deep inside
her. Nadia drew in a sharp breath, her body going rigid,
but then she pushed back up, straddling him, so he plunged
in even deeper, his groan even more feral. In control now,
she raised her hips, steadying herself with her hands on
his abs as he started to thrust, his slick, heated, swollen
member desperate to be satisfied. With Nadia bucking
wildly on top of him he knew he couldn't hold on much
longer, but when she arched back with a moan of pleasure
then fell forward onto his chest with sated exhaustion he
grabbed hold of her buttocks and with a final punishing
thrust he felt himself explode inside her. The release was
extraordinary—a release of intense pressure, of stifled
control, of every damned thing in the world.

# CHAPTER ELEVEN

SEVERAL HOURS HAD PASSED since Zayed and Nadia had
left Azeed's encampment to travel to the palace of Harith.
Nadia knew they must be nearing their destination.

It had been another journey with very limited conversation. Apart from a brief discussion about her brother,
when she had tried to impress upon Zayed the kind of man
Imran was, they had both been virtually silent.

Instead, Nadia had gazed unseeing at the arid plains of
the desert that had flashed past the window, going over in
her head what they had done last night. She should never
have tempted him into bed with her, she knew that, even
before Zayed had extricated himself from her arms at the
first light of dawn. But she had craved the intimacy so
badly, *yearned* for him so badly, that lonely, frightening
night more than ever. It had been a force she had been
powerless to resist.

And now she found herself reliving that amazing intimacy, minute by minute, in all its gloriously erotic pleasure. She was just remembering when Zayed had brought
her to orgasm that first time when the SUV jolted over a
large boulder in their path and she had to stifle the shaft
of arousal that shot through her, biting down hard on her
lip before nervously glancing across at Zayed to see if he
had noticed.

But she needn't have worried. Zayed continued to stare
straight ahead, lost in his own thoughts, his dark hands

gripping the wheel. And Nadia was under no illusions that those thoughts included her.

For while everything about the memory of last night still consumed her, right down to the feel of the rough blankets that had scratched their entwined bodies as they had finally fallen asleep, for Zayed they were already gone, forgotten.

Daylight had seen him revert to his old self. Brisk, formal, businesslike, all vestiges of passion and tenderness gone.

Which just served to remind Nadia of her foolishness. What was it Zayed had said to her after their wedding night? *It was just sex.* His words had scarred her then, and now they weighted her down with their punishing truth.

Because for her it was far more than just sex. Far, far more. With the sickening dread of reality Nadia now realised that it was not just her virginity she had lost to this man. She had lost her heart. And that was something she didn't know how to begin to come to terms with.

The palace of Harith loomed before them, cold and forbidding, despite the searing midday heat. Zayed slanted a look at Nadia as they swung through the arched entranceway into the wide cobbled courtyard, the security gates closing behind them. She looked very pale, her hands gripping the seat, her knuckles white.

'Are you okay?' He pulled up the car and turned off the engine.

'Yes, yes. It's just being back here…you know.'

Zayed turned to look at her, wanting to comfort her but knowing she would never let him. They had briefly stopped at a coffee shop on the outskirts of the city so that he could check in with his security team and to give them both a chance to change out of their dusty clothes. Now he was wearing a sombre suit and tie, Nadia a traditional abaya in a deep shade of blue. She looked beautiful, delicate, fragile.

'You know there is nothing to be frightened of?'

From the brief conversation they had had on the journey he had discovered that, despite the facade of bravado, Nadia feared her brother almost as much as her father. She hadn't said it in so many words, but the way she had turned to look at him, clasping the seat belt against her chest, her eyes wide with alarm, had said it for her.

'You need to be careful with Imran, Zayed. He can be sly, nasty, vicious.'

'Sounds like quite a charmer.'

'I mean it, Zayed.' He had felt her gaze intensify as she had focused on his profile, willing him to understand.

'Frankly, I don't give a damn what he's like.' The fact was he already hated this guy because of the way he had treated Nadia. For the way he made her feel. 'It's not as if I'm planning on watching baseball with him. But if this is my one chance to talk some sense into Imran Amani then I am going to make it count.'

'Yes, of course.' Her eyes had returned to the track in front of them but the disquiet had still been in her voice. 'But you will need to be on your guard. Imran is not an honourable man. Not like your brother.'

*Honourable.* That was the word to describe Azeed, Zayed realised that now. Their talk the previous night had opened his eyes to the changed man his brother had become, the brother he had never really known. And he was so grateful for the bond they now had.

As he had swung the SUV between the towering dunes, deeper and deeper into this enemy territory, he had hoped that being honourable was one quality they had in common.

Now, here in the heart of Harith, he watched as Nadia collected herself, fighting off his concern. She pulled down the sun visor and looked at herself in the mirror, smoothing her hands over her hair, running a fingertip over her eyebrows. Zayed waited until she had finished.

'Nadia?' She turned to look at him and he caught her raised chin with his finger, holding it still. He watched her pupils dilate, the thick dark lashes fluttering.

'Yes?'

'Do you trust me, Nadia?'

He wanted a truthful answer, refusing to let her look away until he'd got one. There were dangers attached to this plan—he knew that. But he also knew that he would protect Nadia with his life. He was prepared to raze the kingdom of Harith to the ground, himself along with it, before he would let anything happen to her.

'Yes, Zayed, I trust you.'

'Thank you.'

That was all he needed to know.

The palace seemed very quiet. A servant, his head bowed so low that he didn't look into their faces, had ushered them into the echoing hallway, and on Zayed's firm announcement that they were here to see Prince Imran had indicated that they should follow him. He led them down a maze of flagstone corridors deep into the heart of the palace before leaving them outside an ancient panelled door. Somewhere in the distance a dog howled.

'Ready?' Zayed asked the question, his knuckles raised in readiness to knock. Nadia nodded, holding herself very still. Zayed rapped on the door.

Imran Amani was seated behind a wooden desk in a sparsely decorated room with a vaulted stone ceiling. At the sight of the two of them he scraped back his chair, leaping to his feet.

'What is the meaning of this?' His dark, hawkish features darted from one to the other, shock at the sight of his sister shaking his composure, shaking his hands, too, as they gripped the edge of the desk. 'What is she doing here?'

'Prince Imran.' Zayed spoke slowly, deliberately. 'Thank you for agreeing to meet with me.'

'Where did you find her?' He pointed at Nadia with a trembling finger. 'What sort of trick is this?'

'No trick, Your Royal Highness. There is no need for you to be alarmed.'

'I'm not alarmed.' His voice rose an octave. 'It is you that should be alarmed. You and that creature you have brought with you.'

Zayed took in the man opposite him. About the same age as himself, he was several inches shorter, with the sort of body that needed a good personal trainer. Was this *really* the man who Nadia feared? One thing was for sure, he wasn't going to speak to her like that.

'Before we go any further I must ask that you show your sister some respect.'

'Respect? You bring this woman here and ask for respect?' Imran Amani tried for a derisive sneer but under Zayed's direct gaze it froze on his face. 'In any event—' he cast about for his lost dignity '—she is no sister of mine. She has brought shame on our family and disgrace to our kingdom.'

'Imran, if you would just listen to what we have to say...' Nadia took a step towards her brother but Zayed stretched out a hand to bar her way. He didn't want her getting too close to this vile man.

'That's right, protect your prey. You may have brought her here to drop like a rat at my feet but you will certainly get no reward.'

The room suddenly went chillingly quiet. Zayed could feel Nadia's eyes on his but he didn't trust himself to look back at her. Because he knew that if he saw the hurt in them he wouldn't be held responsible for his actions. He sucked in a deep breath.

'Prince Imran. I'm sure your sister must be tired after her long journey. Perhaps you would be kind enough to offer her a seat?' Without waiting for a reply he reached for a chair for Nadia and one for himself. Reluctantly Imran Amani acknowledged that they were all sitting down.

'Now.' Zayed spoke with deadly calm. 'Let us continue. I asked my brother to arrange this meeting because—'

'Your brother, yes.' The memory of Azeed sparked another frothing outburst. 'He begged me to meet with you, and this is how you repay my generosity.'

'I asked Azeed to arrange this meeting—' Zayed forced the words through the clench of his jaw '—because there are things we need to discuss.'

'I have nothing to say to you. Or her.'

'Then, perhaps you would like to listen.' Zayed risked a look at Nadia now, sitting silently beside him. Her hands were twisting in her lap, creasing the fabric of her gown. But her head was held high. 'The first thing Nadia and I have to tell you is that we are married.'

Another deadly silence filled the room, Imran Amani opening and closing his mouth like a goldfish.

'Married?' He finally managed to spit out the words. 'To each other.'

'That is correct.' There were no flies on this one. Actually, there would be if Zayed had his way, crawling over his rotting corpse.

'You are married to *Nadia*?' His face was busy going several interesting shades of red.

'It's true, Imran.' Nadia's voice was soft but clear in the hollow emptiness of the room. 'Zayed Al Afzal is my husband.'

Zayed stilled, something about her words laying him bare. Was that the first time he had ever heard her refer to him as her husband?

'No!' Imran Amani was up on his feet again, moving out from behind the desk, then swinging back, a look of evil pleasure crossing his face. 'Well—' there was a childish excitement in his voice '—I can't wait to tell my father the good news. You know he will have you both killed?'

'He will do no such thing.' Zayed rose slowly to his feet.

'Then you don't know our father like we do, does he, Nadia?' He addressed his sister for the first time, now relishing the sibling connection, reverting to the bullying ways of his childhood. 'You have made a very stupid mistake coming back to Harith with this news.' Seeing Zayed's much taller figure looming in front of him, he took a couple of steps back. 'By choosing to share the bed of a man who is ruler of our sworn enemy, Nadia has brought about certain war.'

'I think you will find the reverse is true.' Zayed's voice was calm and measured. 'By choosing to share my bed, as you put it, Nadia has, in all probability, saved your country. Because that is the other reason we are here, Prince Imran. To make peace between our two nations.'

'Peace! Ha! You've got a strange way of going about it.' Imran was hopping about from foot to foot now. 'You have been away from your country for too long, Sheikh Zayed. Your brain is addled by your Western ways. Perhaps you should seek advice from your brother, Azeed. He has courage and spirit, something you know nothing about. He does not fear war like you.'

'You are right, I do fear war.' At Zayed's words Prince Imran's sneer turned into a smile of triumph, but it was short-lived. 'I would hate to see the blood of my countrymen spilled over such a conflict. But mostly I fear war for your kingdom.'

'The kingdom of Harith is fierce and noble. We will never be cowed.'

'The kingdom of Harith is on the point of economic collapse. If you were to go to war with Gazbiyaa, a war you could never win, it would mean not only a deplorable loss of life, but financial ruin, as well.'

'What are these lies that you speak?' Prince Imran paced back to the desk then lunged forward again, beads of sweat on his brow. 'Ah, now I see.' He swung his hate-filled eyes towards Nadia. 'The viper in the nest is right beside you.'

Zayed flexed his biceps. This loathsome man was really asking for it. He was ready, more than ready, to take him down without any further provocation. But as the bile filled his throat, he felt the touch of Nadia's hand on his arm, forcing him to collect himself.

'My background is finance.' He barked the words, keeping it short. He owed this man no explanations. 'I know a country in severe economic difficulties when I see one.'

Imran Amani ran a shaky hand over his brow as he desperately tried to formulate a fitting response. 'We may not have riches,' he finally managed, 'but we have courage and valour. Something that you know nothing about.'

'There is more to courage than beating your chest in a vain attempt to show your might. The real test of courage is to face up to the truth of the situation and have the guts to deal with it.'

'*Pah!* You come crawling in here, hiding behind your wife, no doubt doing her bidding, and dare to speak to me of courage. What real man would do such a thing?'

'My wife is Harithian. That is why we are here. But more than that, Nadia is my equal and I respect her opinion. I suggest you do the same. And just for the record—' he felt the muscles in his neck tighten '—she has more courage in her little finger than you have in the whole of your pathetic, flaccid body.'

'Your wife is nothing more than a common whore.'

That was *it*! In a split second Zayed had lunged at Imran Amani, grabbing him by the scruff of the neck and hauling him up into the air.

'Zayed! No!'

He had his hand on the man's throat, his face right in front of the bulging eyes of his victim. What he wouldn't like to do to him. But Nadia was beside him now, pulling on the sleeve of his jacket. The spoilsport.

'Don't you ever, *ever*, speak of my wife like that again.' Zayed had to content himself with giving the creature a hound-like shake, his voice a deadly growl. 'Do I make myself clear?'

Amani gave a terrified nod.

'Good.' Moving round the desk, he loosened his grip on his brother-in-law and unceremoniously dropped him down in his seat. 'Just as long as we understand each other. Now it is time for you to listen hard and listen good.'

Nadia breathed a sigh of relief. At least they were all sitting down again, for the time being anyway. She knew Zayed well enough to see that he was holding his temper on a very short rein. She knew her brother well enough to see that he was beaten.

She stole a look from one man to the other. Why had she ever doubted that Zayed would be able to deal with Imran? Well, he hadn't so much dealt with him as made mincemeat of him. In fact, if she hadn't stopped him that might literally have been the case. She had *never* seen Zayed so close to real violence, never expected to see him so pumped up and ready to fight. And although his famous control had kicked in before any blood was spilled, she couldn't help the shiver of excitement that went through her when she thought about the way he had leaped to her defence.

Zayed had looked magnificent standing there, effortlessly holding her squirming brother by the neck. This brother that had made her teenage years such a misery, whom she had been ordered to respect, to honour, to obey. Suddenly all the years of oppression fell away, along with the scales from her eyes. She'd never had any intention of doing any of those things anyway, but now she realised she didn't have to like him, let alone love him. He was nothing to her. And she didn't have to feel guilty about that, either.

She realised something else, too. Zayed was the only person who had ever stood up for her. Her father too despotic, her brother too vile, her mother too weak. She had always been on her own, fighting her own cause. It felt so good to have someone on her side. Especially when that someone was Zayed.

He was speaking to her brother now, his voice low and authoritative, spelling out to Imran very clearly what he had to do. There was a veneer of calm about him, but Nadia could see the clench of his jaw beneath the close-cropped beard, the way his hands, resting in his lap with the fingers laced, squeezed as he spoke. The tie round his neck had been wrenched to one side, the sleeves of his jacket pushed up. He meant business. Nadia's heart sighed.

'So when your father returns from his business trip with his begging bowl empty, yes—' he paused in response to Imran's head shooting up from the notepad he had been furiously scribbling on '—I know all about that, too. Trust me, there's not a financial backer in the world that will touch this place. When he returns I suggest you put forward my generous proposals. And you had better make them convincing. Because one day soon you will be sheikh of Harith. Do you want to be ruler of a kingdom growing in wealth and prosperity? Or one decimated by war? How you present the facts to your father is going to seal that fate.'

Imran stole a look at his sister, and, raising her eyebrows, Nadia stared back. It was a silent exchange but it said it all. For the first time ever, Nadia was the victor.

# CHAPTER TWELVE

Sitting at her dressing table, Nadia fastened the gold bracelet around her wrist and, looking up, caught sight of her reflection in the mirror. She leaned in closer. Those were her mother's eyes staring back at her. The same shape, the same deep lilac colour and now holding the same shuttered anxiety. Years of living with Nadia's father had brought about that look in her mother. Zayed had done it to Nadia in a matter of months.

It had been three weeks since they'd returned from Harith, when Nadia had been filled with such hope and optimism. The relief that the threat of war had been lifted was immense, but, more than that, she had somehow managed to convince herself that their relationship might change now, that the wretched wedding contract no longer applied. That there might be the beginnings of a real, true relationship between them.

How foolish she had been.

For with each passing week Zayed had become more cold towards her, more distant, more withdrawn, her misguided optimism dashed against the towering wall of his complete disregard.

She thought back to how proud her mother had been of her when she had briefly seen her in Harith. How proud Nadia had been to introduce Zayed to her and to hear him explain the plans he had put in place to ensure peace between the two kingdoms. Now she felt guilty for deceiving her mother, about their relationship at least. She could already imagine the look of hurt in her eyes when she found out their marriage had been nothing more than a sham.

Zayed's father had also been briefed of the situation, both the negotiations with Prince Imran and the fact that Nadia was, in fact, the daughter of the sheikh of Harith. With Nadia sitting apprehensively beside him Zayed had delivered the information politely but very firmly, and certainly with no apologies. Her father-in-law hadn't exactly tossed his walking stick in the air with joy, but he had at least accepted the news. More than that, he had accepted his son's complete and absolute command.

And that was when Nadia had recognised the change in Zayed. He was now every inch the commanding, powerful ruler. Any lingering resentment he'd had, any yearning for the life he had left in the west, had long gone. He was now the true sheikh of Gazbiyaa. A role he had been unwittingly born for, a role he had finally accepted, a role he was perfect for.

But that brought about a sadness all of its own. Because no matter how much the world around them had improved, the relationship between the two of them could hardly have been worse.

All of which made what Nadia had to tell Zayed tonight so desperately, gut-wrenchingly hard.

Hearing Nadia enter the dining room, Zayed stopped pacing around and turned to look at her. The familiar lurch of desire kicked in.

She was wearing a sleeveless green silk dress that caught the light as she came towards him, her long legs bare, her hair falling loose over her shoulders. She looked poised and solemn and totally beautiful.

Seeing her simply confirmed all his convictions. They couldn't carry on like this. *He* couldn't carry on like this.

Because being around Nadia was driving him completely and utterly crazy.

Every little thing about her set him off, tested his resolve, robbed him of his self-control, tormented him beyond belief. The way she looked, the way she moved, the way she smelled. He found himself conjuring up her little gestures and mannerisms even when they weren't together, just for the tortured fun of it, remembering the way she would touch her earlobe when she was thinking, or bite down on her bottom lip or twist a curl of dark hair between her fingers.

And those eyes… The eyes that were trained on him now, holding him with their steady, lethal power. He had to put an end to this madness. And he would. Tonight.

'Imran has been on the phone again.' He lobbed her brother's name in as a diversionary conversation starter.

'Oh, I'm sorry.' As they sat down Nadia shook open the napkin on her lap, her eyes lowered. 'What did he want this time?'

'Some daft business idea he's got, breeding Arab stallions, would you believe? I had to put him straight, again, that the money Gazbiyaa is investing in his country is to be used for infrastructure, health, education. Certainly not for him to canter about at the races.'

'And you can control that?'

'Too right I can.'

This at least was one aspect of his life that he could control. His little talk with Prince Imran had done the trick and hostilities between the two kingdoms had ceased. Imran Amani had broken the news to his father of Nadia's marriage to Sheikh Zayed, eventually making him see that, far from being a cause for war, it was one for optimism, if not celebration. Because it would save Harith from financial ruin.

The delicate negotiations had necessitated Imran Amani

constantly contacting Zayed for advice, something that Zayed knew he had to put up with but found increasingly hard to tolerate. One thing was for sure: they were never going to be best friends. The guy made his skin crawl.

'My legal team have been all over that Harithian contract. There is no way Amani is going to get his greasy mitts on that money for his personal gain.'

'Zayed—'

'I know, I know. He's your brother and I shouldn't speak about him like that.'

'It's not that. There's something I need to talk to you about, something we need to discuss.'

Zayed raised his eyes from the meal he was concentrating so assiduously on, that he had no appetite for. There was a catch in her voice that drew his gaze to her face. She looked tired, he realised, paler than usual but with faint dark shadows under her eyes.

This wasn't easy for her, either, was it? He was so busy thinking about himself, about how he felt, that it had only just occurred to him how uncharacteristically quiet Nadia had been for the past few days. Or maybe he had refused to notice. Because maybe that quietness was her plotting how she could get away from him, be rid of him. After all, she had achieved her aim, all that she cared about: finding peace and security for Harith. Why would she want to hang around here now? There was the little matter of their marriage, of course, but that would be sorted in due course. In the meantime he could offer her a way out. One that might just save his sanity.

'I know what you are going to say.' He felt the sharp dart of her gaze, heard her fork rattle against her plate. 'And I agree. There is no reason for you to have to stay in the palace now.'

'I'm sorry?'

'Until we can proceed with the divorce there are a number of other properties you could use. Or failing that, perhaps you would like to spend some time in Harith?'

'Harith?' *Why was she doing this? Feigning surprise, looking at him as if he were the bad guy? Wasn't this hard enough already?*

'Yes. You could help with some of the administrative stuff.' She stared at him. 'I don't know, whatever, be more hands-on if that's what you want.' Impatience hardened his words now, her baffling reluctance to accept what he was saying seriously winding him up.

'You want me to go and live in Harith?'

'I am saying that you have served your penance.' He glared back at her. 'There is no longer any need for you to stay here in the palace with me. The prison gates are open.' He gestured with a wide-armed sweep. 'You are free to go whenever you want.'

'I see.' Her voice was very low, small. 'And if I don't want to go?'

*What was she trying to do to him?* It was obvious how much she disliked him; it was written all over her face. From the dark frown that lowered her brows to the pulse that beat in her throat, like the twitch of a cat's tail. Or the way she pursed together those soft pink lips, holding back whatever home truths she wanted to spit at him.

What did she possibly have to gain from being difficult now, except perhaps to torture him further? Well, two could play at that game.

'I am obviously not making myself clear.' Pushing his plate away, Zayed turned in his seat to give Nadia the full force of his steely gaze. 'As of now, Nadia, our wedding contract is terminated. I want you out of the palace and out of my life.'

There was a moment of heartbreaking stillness.

Zayed watched the flush slowly creeping up Nadia's neck, her fingers trembling as they sought to halt it.

'Fine.' Suddenly she was up on her feet, the plates and glasses on the table rattling in protest as her hands gripped the cloth beneath them. She stiffened her spine, pulled herself up to as much height as she could muster.

'But just before you fling me out onto the streets perhaps there is one thing I should tell you.'

Zayed waited, something about the look on Nadia's face snaring the breath in his chest.

'I am pregnant.'

Time stopped.

Nadia stared at the man before her. Her every deep-rooted fear, every gnawing dread now realised in the black depths of Zayed's eyes.

He was horrified. Appalled. Aghast. So devastated that he couldn't even speak. All the things she had known he would be when she had held that tester stick in her hand and stared at the two pink lines.

'Pregnant?'

'Yes.'

'You're sure?'

'Quite sure.' Of course she was sure. She had known even before she'd done the test, immediately sensing the changes in her body when her period was no more than a couple of days late.

'Hell!' Zayed leaped to his feet, turning away from her before swinging back with a look of bitter desperation. 'That night in the desert?'

Nadia nodded stiffly.

'How could I have been such a fool?' He covered his eyes with his hand, blocking Nadia out from his private turmoil, as if he was trying to make her disappear.

Well, she would, if that was what he wanted. Nadia gripped the back of her chair as she stared at the tormented figure before her. Her hands were shaking, her whole body in danger of joining in as a chill of dread swept over her. It was a dread that clawed at her with its icy fingers, pointing out the terrible truth. The dread of realisation that she meant nothing to him.

Because, despite everything, until now Nadia had still hoped. A tiny part of her, a little kernel of optimism, had been clinging to the belief that maybe this news didn't have to be so disastrous. Maybe Zayed would embrace the idea, maybe he would even embrace her, tell her everything would be all right. Now that foolish optimism lay raw and bleeding at her feet. The word *disastrous* didn't even beginning to describe his reaction. There wasn't a word in the English language hideous enough for that. Or for the way she was feeling right now.

For not only had Zayed's reaction told Nadia how he felt about her, it had confirmed how *she* felt about *him*. And it was that that unfurled the curl of misery inside her now, twisting its way brutally past her internal organs until it found its true victim—her heart. Where it mercilessly wrapped its tendrils around and around, its grip so tight that Nadia knew there would never be any release.

She loved Zayed. Loved him with an all-consuming certainty. Like breathing, it was a love so fundamental, so basic, that at first she had hardly noticed it; it was just a part of who she was. Or maybe she had refused to notice it because, like breathing, to focus on it only caused an anxiety that she hadn't known was there. Except, of course, she had known. She had most probably known from the very first moment she had seen him. When she had skidded into the stateroom wearing that loathsome outfit and been met by his deep, dark, searchingly beautiful eyes. But it was a love she had refused to acknowledge, even to herself, because she had known it would never be reciprocated, had known that she was totally alone with this one. She was in the dark and claustrophobic tunnel of love and there was no one sitting beside her.

She could feel the force of those eyes on her now, still searching, only this time they were cold and harsh, searching for a way out of this appalling mess. Because that was obviously how he viewed it—their marriage and their baby. Yet another massive problem that had to be dealt with.

Well, she refused to be his problem any more. She was done with that. Now she had to dig deep, deeper than she ever had before, to find the determination, the self-preservation, to get her through this. Her fighting spirit was her only weapon, but it was well honed.

Years of suffering injustice and prejudice at the hands of her father and brother had seen to that. She had refused to bend to their will and she had won. Now she had another battle to fight, the hardest battle of her life. There would be no victors, that was for sure. But she *had* to protect herself from this onslaught of pain. Protect herself and protect her baby, their baby, that was growing inside her now. It was only a scrap of life at the moment, a miracle of dividing cells, but Nadia loved it already. The baby was her future. It would be her strength.

'We are both equally responsible for what has happened.' She fumbled her way back down onto her seat, fighting to control her trembling body, to stop him from seeing the agony she was feeling. 'But please don't feel you have to be responsible for anything else. If my *penance is served*—' she quoted his phrase back at him, her voice hollow with effort '—then so is yours. I will do as you say, go back to Harith and have the baby there. You need have nothing more to do with me. With either of us.'

'Don't be so ridiculous.' Zayed glared down at her, his fists balled by his sides, impotent anger pumping through him. 'I didn't know you were pregnant when I suggested you went back to Harith. Obviously that changes everything. Now we are tied together forever.'

*Tied together forever.* Like a ball and chain. A life sentence.

'No, you are wrong. I will take full responsibility for the baby. You can still have your freedom. You can still have your divorce.'

'And you really think you could do that?'

'Yes, yes, I do. The baby and I will be fine. We can manage perfectly well without you.' She had to keep up the pretence, hold on to the bravado.

'I can see I need to rephrase that.' Zayed pulled up a chair and sat down heavily in front of her, leaning forward for emphasis, the harsh angled planes of his face just inches from hers. 'When I said did you think you *could* do that I meant did you think I would *let* you do that.'

Of course. How could she have got that wrong? How could she have thought that just for one moment he might have been looking at this through her eyes?

Drawing in a deep, shuddering breath, she struggled to stop herself from screaming or fainting or a pathetic flailing combination of the two. She was a fighter. She would not let herself collapse before him.

'It is not up to you to tell me what I can do or where I can go.'

'I think you will find that it is.' His voice was chillingly clear. 'You are my wife, the sheikha of Gazbiyaa. And you are carrying my child. You will do as I say.'

They stared at each other in total silence as the realisation of what he had said glinted between them, sharp and jagged, like the teeth of a saw.

So it was out there. Nadia had come full circle. By escaping the rule of one tyrannical family she had ended up shackled to another.

A *family*. It was the first time she had thought of them as a family: she, Zayed and the baby. Now that word, that image, all but broke her heart.

She dragged her gaze away from his, from the sheer miserable sadness of it all. She wanted to howl or wail or beat at him with her fists to try to get through to him. To show him what he had done to her.

But she wouldn't do any of those things. Because she still had her pride. Grimly clinging on to that alone, she pushed herself up from the chair.

'I am not prepared to discuss this any further.' Standing tall now, she jutted back her shoulders to deliver one last, harrowing stare before turning on her heel.

'Oh, no, you don't.' Zayed was behind her in an instant, his hand gripping the back of her arm. 'Don't think you can just run away from me.'

Nadia turned into the granite wall of his chest, inhaling his masculine scent, his barely leashed power. It all but knocked her legs from under her. 'I have never run away from anything in my life.' As she angled her face up at him she felt her knees wobble, rubber where cartilage and bone had once been. She had to get out before she literally fell at his feet. 'But right now I need to be on my own.'

And with that she turned and stumbled from the room.

# CHAPTER THIRTEEN

ZAYED WATCHED NADIA'S departing figure, so desperate to get away from him that she was tripping over her feet, reaching out to the door frame for support.

*Pregnant.* How the hell could he have let this happen? How could he have been so careless? He who prided himself on his self-control at all times, his measured approach, the shrewd, calculating head on his shoulders. His friends might have ribbed him for it, but they relied on it, too, especially Stefan, whose hot-headed temper had been cooled by the practical Zayed many times over the years.

But the mess he'd got himself into now was worthy of the most moronic of men, and the anger at his stupidity surpassed anything that Stefan could have thrown at him. It boiled inside him, heating his core with its molten power.

What the hell had happened to his life?

Nadia. That was what had happened. Since the second she had appeared before him in that ridiculous outfit his life had gone off the rails. And all his efforts to stop the runaway train had ultimately been futile.

Raising his hands to his eyes, he pushed his knuckles hard against his closed lids, letting the flashes of light blot out the world for a second.

*Pregnant.* The shocking news had hit him like a hammer blow to the head. He was going to be a father. Something he had vowed never to let happen, deciding long ago that he didn't want the responsibility of bringing a child into this world. He had never wanted to marry, either, come to that. His parents' fractured marriage had been more than enough to put him off that idea for life, and the fraught relationship it had fostered with his brother only confirming that marriage and kids were definitely not for him. He hadn't been able to get out of that particular hothouse of tensions fast enough.

And now here he was, back in Gazbiyaa, married and soon to be a father. The three things that up until a few months ago he would have sworn never would happen.

Like falling in love.

The words flew, unbidden, into his head and lodged there, refusing to budge, wilful and persistent. Was that what had happened to him? Was that why he had lost control of his life, of his head, of every flaming part of his body?

He was in love with Nadia. Zayed turned the startling realisation over in his head. Of all the women he could have fallen in love with, of all the eligible, beautiful, uncomplicated women he might have chosen, the only one who had burrowed deep inside him and captured his stubborn, untouched heart was Nadia. No one had ever challenged him like Nadia; no one had ever made him feel the way Nadia did. And there was the irony. For Nadia was the one women he could guarantee would never love him back.

He stared at the empty doorway, picturing the expression on her face when she had left. He shouldn't have let her go, not like that. When she had told him she was pregnant his reaction had been cruel, heartless. He hadn't even considered how she might be feeling. Shock had played a part, but it didn't excuse his despicable behaviour.

He should have handled the situation so much better. He *definitely* shouldn't have done the heavy-handed 'you will do as I say' routine. That was as good as guaranteeing she would do the opposite. A cold thought ran through him like the blade of a stiletto. Supposing she was planning on leaving? Tonight.

He had to find her, right away. He had to try to make amends, to stop her from doing anything stupid. He might not be able to make her love him but he could stop behaving like a jerk.

With his feet pounding along the echoing corridors he headed for the palace courtyard, Nadia's favourite bolthole, a huge surge of relief washing over him when he realised he had guessed right; she was there. She had her back to him, sitting on one of the benches under an archway, hunched over with her arms wrapped around her knees.

Relief made way for pain. She looked so small. So alone. He wanted to take her in his arms and try to make everything right. If only he could.

The trickle of water in the rill disguised the sound of his footsteps, and he was right behind her before she realised he was there, the light touch of his hand on her shoulder making her leap sideways. She shot him a lightning glance before looking away again, but it was enough for Zayed to see that she had been crying.

'Nadia?'

'Go away.'

'Nadia.' He walked round her until he was in front of her and, sitting down on the bench, lowered his head, trying to look into her face. Nadia went to swivel round the other way but he caught her shoulders in his strong grasp and held her firm. 'We need to talk.'

'I have nothing to say to you.' The words were gulped between swallowed sobs. 'Go away and leave me alone.'

'No. I'm not going anywhere until you have heard what I have to say.' He watched as a fat tear escaped and rolled down her cheek. The sight of it nearly crucified him. Reaching forward, he stopped its progress with his finger, feeling its wetness on his skin. Nadia's tear. He had never seen her cry before, no matter how dangerous or frightening the situation. And she had already faced far too many of them.

But now as he moved his hand beneath her jaw, as she raised her heavy-lidded eyes to meet his, the tears began to flow freely, silently, chasing each other down the side of her nose, down her cheeks, dripping into her mouth and from her chin. In true Nadia style, she never did anything in half measures. Cupping her face in his hands, Zayed felt them pooling into his palms, running down his forearms, more and more, as if they would never stop. His heart tugged inside him.

'Nadia.' What had he done to her? Pulling her body into a stiff embrace, he wrapped his arms around her, pinning her to his chest. Her sobs shuddered between them, each jarring jolt torturing him more than the last as the depths of her misery became ever clearer. 'I'm so sorry.' He whispered the words into her hair, inhaling the scent of her, the feel of her.

He felt her move inside his arms like a small trapped creature, struggling feebly against the ring of his embrace that he had no intention of releasing. Finally she went quiet again and when she tried to raise her head he let her, looking down at her face, wet with tears, drained but still defiant. Still beautiful.

'I don't want your apologies, Zayed.' The fight was returning to her now, arching her spine. 'In fact, I don't want anything from you. But I do want this baby, and I will raise it on my own if I have to. In fact I would rather raise it on my own than subject it to life with a father who didn't want it, who resented it, who couldn't find it in his heart to—'

Lowering his head, he covered her open mouth with his own, halting her words with his lips, breathing in her anger and her anguish, taking them away from her the only way he knew how. With a searing kiss.

Nadia's body, tense and rigid in his arms, slowly loosened and leaned into his, and that was all the encouragement he needed to deepen the kiss still further, to feel her more intensely. With the faintest of moans she started to respond, to give in to him, to the incredibly powerful connection between them. The fire and passion that never went away, no matter how much they fought or fell out or tried to deny it. The passion that had made a baby, a new life, that was growing inside Nadia now. Suddenly Zayed realised how incredible that was. How utterly, astonishingly amazing.

But the thought was short-lived, wrenched away by Nadia's sudden movement as she jerked back her head, gasping for breath and struggling to get away from him again. 'Let me go!' Her hands were trying to find purchase against the wall of his chest, her hair a mess of dark curls, her breasts rising and falling, crushed between them.

Tightening his hold, Zayed trapped her flailing hands and held them against him, his eyes never leaving Nadia's flushed and tear-stained face. He stared down at her, at the lips swollen from the force of his kiss, the thick strand of hair falling across her cheekbone, the clumps of wet eyelashes, weighting her eyelids as she blinked back at him, framing those extraordinary, beautiful eyes. 'I'm not going to let you go until you promise you will listen to me.'

'Well, we will be here a long time, then.' Defiant to the last, Nadia struggled in his arms with renewed effort. 'Because I don't want to hear anything you have to say.'

'Well, that's too bad, because you are going to hear it anyway.'

'Fine. But I warn you, it won't make the slightest bit of difference. I already know exactly how you feel about me, and now the baby, too, so don't even bother to try to—'

'I love you, Nadia.'

The stunned silence was filled with a rumble of thunder from above, as if his words had awoken the very gods in the skies.

'No.' Releasing her body from the imprisonment of his chest, Nadia leaped to her feet, taking several steps away. Zayed stood up to face her, tall, dark, rigid with tension.

Rain was pouring down now, a vertical torrent of water, bouncing off the mosaic tiles of the courtyard, flooding the peaceful rill. From beneath their archway Nadia and Zayed stared at one another.

'No.' Nadia repeated the word, shaking her head. She said something else, her lips moving but the noise of the rain drowning out her voice. Zayed moved closer, fighting the dread in his heart. He knew this was going to be bad, hideously bad, but he had committed himself now. Laid himself bare. And despite the pain, the certainty that his declaration would bring him nothing but misery, it was a relief to have gotten it off his chest. To have spoken the words out loud.

'You are wrong.' She was shouting now, her voice high and shrill over the pounding, deafening rain, desperate to make him hear, to understand. 'You don't love me.'

Closing the gap between them, Zayed took her face in his hands, holding it still. 'I love you, Nadia.' He mouthed the words clearly, so that there could be no mistake. Then, reaching to tuck her hair behind one ear, he moved his lips against the soft pink folds and said it again. 'I love you.' This time it whispered into her eardrum, down into her very soul.

Nadia stood perfectly still, holding on to this one little perfect moment in time. Because it couldn't last; it wasn't possible. The sledgehammer of reality had to kick in any moment now. With her face still held in his hands Zayed was looking deep into her eyes, searching them for clues, waiting for her to respond.

'Nadia?' He spoke her name over the drumbeat of rain,

permeating the fog of her mind, anguish now shadowing his face, darkening the eyes that still held hers.

She knew she needed to say something, anything, to take away that pain. But somehow the words wouldn't come. She couldn't push them past her throat. She didn't even know what they were. She felt stunned, numb, weak.

'That's okay.' Dropping his hands, he touched a finger to her twitching lips, shooting her one last, heart-melting look. 'Your silence has said it all.'

Turning away, he stepped out from under the archway and into the torrent of rain, striding off into the curtain of water. He was soaked within a second, his shirt plastered against his back, his hair flattened against his skull.

'Zayed, wait!' Her strangled cry stopped him and he turned back to look at her, water streaming into his eyes, from his chin, sluicing the bunched muscles of his arms and chest. 'Wait for me.'

'No.' He started to run towards her, to stop her. 'Stay there, you mustn't come out in this...'

But it was too late, she had already leaped out into the deluge. The shock of the rain made her gasp, arrowing painfully down on her head and shoulders, almost knocking her over with its force.

Zayed was in front of her now, his arms around her, strong and powerful, holding her steady.

'What the hell do you think you're doing?' He was futilely trying to shelter her with his body, one arm slung over her shoulder, his head bent against the rain as he half dragged her towards the palace.

'Wait.' Pushing herself back against him, Nadia managed to halt his progress. 'I want you to say it again.'

'What?'

'What you said before. Say it again. Please.'

They stared at each other, their hair and faces running with rivulets of water, the soaked clothes on their bodies sticking to their skin, their feet standing in inches of floodwater.

Zayed hesitated, struggling with his pride. Then, taking a step back, he stretched out his arms, tipped his face up to the sky and, filling his lungs with air, bellowed up into the storm, 'I love you, Nadia Al Afzal.'

Nadia moved towards him, slipping her arms around his waist, resting her cheek against his sodden chest. She felt his muscles shift beneath her embrace, his arms fall by his sides.

'That's good.' Looking up, she searched for his eyes through the bouncing rain. 'Because I love you, too.'

Suddenly his lips came down on hers with a bruising, searing kiss that sealed them together. With his mouth still on hers Zayed hooked one arm under Nadia's legs and, lifting her off her feet, dashed towards the shelter of the palace with her body bumping against his. Pausing only to crash in through the door, they hurried to find each other's lips again. It was a kiss that neither of them could bear to let go.

'Are you awake?'

'No.'

Zayed pulled Nadia's naked body even closer to him, stretching one leg over her thigh, nudging his groin against hers. 'And neither should you be.' Reaching an arm out, he lifted the rumpled covers back over them, and Nadia snuggled into him.

Several hours had passed since they had run in from the rain. Their wet clothes were still puddled on the bathroom floor where they had been tugged and dragged off each other's bodies before they had stepped together under the pummelling heat of the shower.

They had been the best several hours of Nadia's life. Without question. Without compare. And close cross-examination of the man by her side had revealed that he felt the same. Even if he was now begging to be allowed to sleep.

She let her fingers trail down over his buttocks, feeling them clenching under her touch.

'Nadia!'

So this was what true happiness felt like. She was consumed by it, filled with it so that she was sure she must be twice her normal size. It was the certainty of it that thrilled her, the way she knew it was forever. Not just the glorious happiness of the past few hours of mind-blowing sexual intimacy, but the knowledge that this was it, the future. Nadia and Zayed. And the baby. Happiness encapsulated.

'I still can't believe that you hid it so well.' She slipped her arms back around Zayed's waist, whispering against his chest, 'I really thought you hated me.'

'Never.' He breathed the word softly into her hair. 'Although hating would have been easy. It was loving you that I found so hard. Losing my heart to the most infuriating, exasperating woman I have ever met.'

'Thank you.'

'You're welcome. But you didn't exactly make it easy for me to accept the truth. I always thought you hated me, too.' Zayed hugged her body tightly. 'I suppose we were both as bad as each other. Now, how about we get some sleep?'

'In a minute. So when did you finally realise how you felt?'

'Hmm…' Zayed sleepily considered her question. 'It wasn't until you told me about the baby that I made myself face up to the stark reality. I knew then that I had to confess my true feelings to you, no matter how hideous the consequences might be for my pride. Or for my heart.'

'Oh, Zayed.' Nadia stirred in his arms, turning so she could kiss his chest where his heart pulsed beneath. 'I really had no idea.'

'I know. But the truth has found its way out now, and that's all that matters.'

'And the baby?' Raising her head, Nadia sought the reassurance of his eyes. 'You're sure…'

'I couldn't be more sure. Or more proud. We are going to make great parents, I just know it.'

'Me, too. And your father will be pleased to hear the news, especially if we manage to produce the future sheikh of Gazbiyaa.'

'He will. Your family, too, I should think. An heir will only forge closer bonds between our two kingdoms now that the ridiculous feud is over. Not that I care whether this is the future sheikh or not.' Zayed pushed his hand down between their sealed bodies and splayed it across Nadia's flat stomach. 'Boy or girl, this is the start of our family, yours and mine. From now on this is about us.'

'Agreed,' Nadia murmured happily. 'But would you mind if we went to Harith to give my parents the news in person? I'd love to be with my mother when we tell her.'

'Of course. As soon as you like.'

'And maybe my mother could come back with us, just for a visit? I know she would never leave my father for long, but it would be so lovely to be able to give her a break, to show her Gazbiyaa, the life we have here.'

'You can bring the entire palace back with you if you like,' Zayed offered. 'Even that brother of yours.'

'Imran?' Nadia laughed softly. 'Surely not?'

'Yep. Even Imran. That's how much I love you, Nadia.'

'Then tell me one more time.'

'I love you, Nadia. I will always love you. Now and forever, with no end.'

All was quiet.

'Nadia?' Zayed gave her a gentle nudge. 'I think you will find it's your turn.'

But Nadia's breathing had turned to a soft snore and,

with her heart beating against his chest and her arms locked around his waist, Zayed knew there would be no reply forthcoming. Shifting slightly, he felt her sigh with contentment.

And that was all the confirmation he needed.

\* \* \* \* \*

*Look out for other titles in the*
SOCIETY WEDDINGS *quartet*
*available now!*

*Late spring, 2016*

'THANK YOU ALL so much for coming.'

Stepping out of the chapel into the bright Greek sunlight, Christian slung his arms over the shoulders of his friends Stefan and Zayed, who were walking on either side of him. 'Alessandra and I are so pleased to have you all here today.'

'Well, we weren't going to miss it, were we?' Stefan slanted him a smile. 'The christening of the first progeny of the Columbia Four.'

'I know. Though I would have understood if you and Nadia hadn't made it, Zayed.' Christian looked across at his friend. 'What with Nadia about to produce your own little *moro* at any moment, I mean.'

'Not long now,' Zayed agreed. 'But believe me, Nadia was adamant that she was coming today. She'd have brought her obstetrician over on the plane with us if necessary.'

'Well, I really appreciate it.'

'And as the only godfather, I obviously had to be here.' Rocco leaned into the conversation. 'I hope you two have noticed my elevated status.'

'Yeah, we've noticed.' Stefan and Zayed exchanged a

smirk. 'It goes with his elevated ego, wouldn't you say, Zayed?'

'Boys, boys.' Christian patted their shoulders. 'You know I would have had all three of you as godfathers to my firstborn, but Alessandra wanted to keep it simple. And as Rocco is her brother...'

'And he's pretty simple...'

'The perfect candidate.'

'Right, *i miei amici*—' Rocco looked from Stefan to Zayed, Christian grinning in between '—if either of you want to be considered as a godparent to my firstborn, you had better start to be more respectful.'

'I think we are going to be spoiled for choice for that role. Must be your turn next to organise a christening, isn't it, Stefan?' Zayed asked.

'Yes, Clio's on it. Unless seeing your daughter being lowered into that font has put her off the idea of getting our baby baptised at all, Christian. She was clutching Tony to her chest as if he might be wrenched away from her and dunked there and then.'

'I did no such thing.' Clio quickened her step to catch up with the men. 'I know that's the tradition here.'

'But you are glad that in Tony's case it will be a little less hard core?'

'No!' Clio laughed, looking down at the sleeping bundle in her arms, shading his head with her hand. 'Though I must admit a mother's urge to protect her child is a pretty powerful one.'

'And a father's, too.' Christian turned to look at Alessandra, who was surrounded by a group of women cooing over the star of the show, his daughter, Letizia, held in his wife's arms. 'It's an amazing feeling, to see your child coming into the world, this whole new life that you have created, so vulnerable but so full of potential. It's like nothing else. What...?'

'Nothing!' Olivia and Nadia had fallen into step with the group, not bothering to hide their amusement. 'We were just thinking how nice it is to see you guys bonding over the baby stuff, weren't we, Nad? Sharing your experiences with our husbands. It's lovely.'

'Then stop smirking, you minxes. I'll have you know The Columbia Four have always been in touch with their feminine sides.'

'Yeah, right, of course you have.' Clio turned to transfer her baby son to her husband before linking arms with Nadia and Olivia. 'It just took a little nudge from us before you all found it.'

'Well, maybe you've got a point there.' Zayed directed a loving glance at his wife and Nadia smiled back, unconsciously smoothing a hand over her sizable baby bump.

The tender exchange reminded the women of the journey they had been on to reach the happiness of today, Alessandra and Christian, too. Because it hadn't been easy for any of them, all of the couples battling heartache and anguish along the way. Perhaps it was inevitable, given the clash of four independent, spirited women coming up against the four ultimate alpha males! But one thing was for sure: if the journey had been torturous, the end result was so worth it. Because these couples had found that rarest of things—true love. And it shone from the eyes of each and every one of them.

'So come on, then.' Zayed turned back to his friends. 'You two are the experienced dads now. Any tips for me and Rocco?'

'*Si*. Make the most of an unbroken night's sleep while you can.' Stefan rocked the stirring baby in his arms. 'Wouldn't you agree, Christian?'

'*Sigoura*—definitely.' Christian nodded in agreement. 'My daughter has certainly reacquainted me with the pleasure of watching dawn break.'

'Sleepless Knights of Columbia?' Nadia ventured, and the whole group burst out laughing.

'What am I missing?' Alessandra and her daughter joined them, baby Letizia looking completely gorgeous in her designer christening gown. 'You are not allowed to have so much fun until I can join in.'

'Well, you're here now, that's the important thing.' Olivia gave her sister-in-law a kiss on the cheek. 'I say the party starts now.'

They had reached the end of the chapel pathway where a fleet of limousines was parked, the doors being opened by their chauffeurs in readiness to transport the guests back to Christian and Alessandra's beautiful home for the celebration lunch.

'Just one second.' Transferring Letizia into the nearest arms, which happened to be a startled Zayed's, Alessandra delved into her bag for her camera. 'Let's have a photo first. If you could all just group together, that's it. Zayed, can you turn so I can see Letizia's face? Yes, and stop looking as if you are holding an unexploded bomb. Now, Stefan, if you—'

'Alessandra!' Her husband lowered his voice for dramatic effect.

'Sorry, *scusa*. Okay.' With a final adjustment to the camera lens, she turned and handed it to an unsuspecting guest behind them. 'Would you mind? If you just look through here and press this. *Grazie mille.*'

Darting back to join the posed group, Alessandra squeezed up next to them. 'Ready, everybody? Smile.'

And smile they did as the camera shutter clicked. Framing their complete happiness forever.

# STEFAN AND CLIO'S WEDDING DAY
# THROUGH THE EYES OF
# SHEIKH ZAYED AL AFZAL

'IF YOU WANT to leave all this behind, leave Stefan behind, then all you have to do is say so, Clio.'

They were standing in the doorway of The Terrace Room of the Chatsfield Hotel, where a room full of New York's most influential and elite guests were awaiting their grand entrance. But as far as Zayed was concerned, they could wait. First he needed to make sure Clio knew she didn't have to go through with this.

Reaching for her bare arm, he tucked it under his elbow in the traditional manner of a man about to give away a bride. But that was where the tradition ended. Because he wasn't going to take another step forward until he had said his piece.

Nothing about this wedding felt right. Not the speed with which it had been arranged, the dismissive way Stefan had refused to discuss it and now, most of all, the way Clio stood rigidly beside him, gripping that bouquet of lilies so tightly in her hands that he half expected them to droop their heads in protest.

The marriage of Stefan and Clio. Stefan, one of Zayed's closest friends, who along with Christian and Rocco made up the inseparable band of brotherhood known as The Columbia Four, and Clio, lovely, funny, clever Clio, who they had all known since university. It should have been cause for massive celebration. A decade ago it would have been. It had been no secret back then that Stefan had had a thing for Clio, providing a source of great entertainment for Zayed and his equally cruel comrades as Clio had continually rejected Stefan's advances and they had seized every opportunity to point that out to their big-headed but baffled friend.

Despite that, ten years ago, the three of them would have been thrilled to see Stefan and Clio come together as a couple. Back then they were well matched. Perfectly matched, even.

But now… Now everything felt different. Wrong. The intervening years had seen Clio distance herself from her university friends. For whatever reason, she'd pulled away, ignoring all invitations to meet up. Even refusing to attend Rocco and Olivia's wedding.

And the years had changed Stefan, too. He was harder, more ruthless, a more brutal man than he had ever been before. With a jolt of alarm Zayed realised that he wouldn't want to see any woman marry the Stefan of today. Least of all Clio. The dear friend he was just about to *give away* to him.

Through a clenched jaw he heard himself whispering with a suppressed urgency that even took him by surprise. He had to make Clio see that she had choices, explain to her that this wedding didn't have to happen, that she could be out of here, whisked away to anywhere in the world she wanted to go—she only had to say the word.

But when Clio turned to look at him, Zayed knew that his impassioned words had fallen on deaf ears.

Not that the smile she'd pasted on fooled him for one moment. In fact if she held it much longer it was in danger of cracking and falling like scales from her unnaturally pale skin.

Neither did her attempt to be lighthearted, as she teased him about his newly acquired royal status and casually probed the depth of his loyalty to Stefan.

But something about the tilt of her chin, the distant look in her eyes as Zayed persisted in trying to make her see sense, told him that he was wasting his breath. That whatever was going on between Stefan and Clio was just that—*between Stefan and Clio*.

'He did not force me into anything, Zayed. This was my choice.'

Clio spoke the words firmly, her cut-glass English accent giving weight to their meaning. She seemed determined that he should understand.

And he wanted to believe her, really he did. But as he patted the hand that she had reached across to find his, her alabaster-cold touch did nothing to allay his deep-rooted fears about this marriage.

If nothing else he would make sure that she knew he was there for her, no matter what, and not just him, Rocco and Christian, too, and their wives. That much he could do. They were all as uneasy about this surprise wedding as he was, the little time they had managed to spend with the *happy couple* the past few days doing little to reassure them.

'You have friends, Clio. Always remember that.'

He watched as Clio smiled back at him through the bright sheen of tears, his heart full of anguished frustration.

'Clio?'

Collecting herself, she hid behind the manners of her breeding, choosing to ignore the pointed meaning behind his statement.

So be it. Zayed squared his shoulders. If this was what Stefan and Clio wanted, he would just have to go along with it. Now it was his turn to paste on the false smile.

'Are you ready for him, Clio?'

They both turned to look at the bridegroom. Standing tall and proud, he silently commanded the respect of the room. And he stared right back at them.

'I'm ready, Zayed,' she whispered.

With a nod of his head the music struck up, and together they moved forward into the room, each step taking them closer and closer to the steely-eyed gaze of Stefan Bianco.

# HARLEQUIN

## *Presents®*

A stunning conclusion to Carol Marinelli's latest
duet, ***Playboys of Sicily***, packed full of fiery passion,
dangerous temptation and heart-stopping excitement!

### His until midnight…?

Losing her virginity to millionaire Matteo Santini came
at a high price for chambermaid Bella—unable to leave
Sicily with Matteo the next day, she lost her heart *and*
her one chance at happiness that night…

But now Matteo's back and more irresistible than ever!
Thrown together at Sicily's most exclusive wedding,
their sizzling attraction still burns bright, and as the
clock strikes midnight, it's clear the only way Bella will
be leaving the party is with Matteo—via his bed!

Find out what happens next in:

# *HIS SICILIAN CINDERELLA*
## *AUGUST 2015*

### Stay Connected:

www.Harlequin.com

www.IHeartPresents.com

 **f** /HarlequinBooks

🐦 @HarlequinBooks

📌 /HarlequinBooks

HP13361